D0117916

Five-Minute Tales

More Stories to Read and Tell When Time Is Short

Margaret Read MacDonald

August House Publishers, Inc.
ATLANTA

For Liz and Ted Parkhurst,
whose love of the storyteller's voice
has honored our tales for twenty-plus years.
Thank you for your dedication to our art.

Copyright © 2007 by Margaret Read MacDonald.
All rights reserved. This book, or parts thereof,
may not be reproduced in any form without permission.

Published 2007 by August House Publishers, Inc.,
3500 Piedmont Road NE, Suite 310, Atlanta, GA 30305
404–442–4420
http://www.augusthouse.com

Book design by Liz Lester

Manufactured in the United States
10 9 8 7 6 5 4 3 2 1   HC
10 9 8 7 6 5 4 3 2 1   PB

LIBRARY OF CONGRESS CATALOGING-IN-PUBLICATION DATA

MacDonald, Margaret Read, 1940–
    Five-minute tales : more stories to read and tell when time is short /
Margaret Read MacDonald.
        p.   cm.
    Includes bibliographical references and index.
    ISBN-13: 978-0-87483-781-0 (hardcover : alk. paper)
    ISBN-13: 978-0-87483-782-7 (pbk. : alk. paper)
    1. Tales. 2. Short story. I. Title.
    GR74.M327   2007
    398.2—dc22
                                        2007014511

The paper used in this publication meets the minimum requirements
of the American National Standards for Information Sciences—
Permanence of Paper for Printed Library Materials, ANSI.48–1984.

ACKNOWLEDGMENTS

Thanks to the many friends and tellers who have shared or enabled the tales in this book:

Naomi Baltuck, Mary Banbury, Nikoloz Baratashivili, Maggie Bennett, Jeffrey Brewster, Murti Bunanta, Inta Carpenter, Loralee Cooley, Livia de Almeida, Elvira DiGiacomo, Irakli Garibashvili, Ketevan Gviniashvili, Martha Hamilton and Mitch Weiss, Joe Hayes, JonLee Joseph, Wendy Kennedy, Kongdeuane Nettavong, Lela Kiana Oman, Uraiwan Prabipu, Marilyn Ribe, Prasong Saihong, Chanphen Singphet, Masako Sueyoshi, Irakli Topuria, Wajuppa Tossa, Supaporn Vathanaprida, Nat Whitman, and Glenda Williams.

CONTENTS

INTRODUCTION

When I prepared the book *Three-Minute Tales* (Little Rock: August House, 2004), my editor, Liz Parkhurst, told me that some of those stories were just flat-out too long. She pointed out that while I—with my rapid-fire delivery—might tell those stories in three minutes, for most folks they would take five.

So she set aside some of the longer tales and asked to add more tales for a second book: *Five-Minute Tales*. Well, with my penchant for telling too fast, it is likely that some of the stories in *this* collection are *seven*-minute tales! But most will come in for most tellers at around five minutes, I think.

Some of the stories in this book are much shorter than five minutes. The section of "Tiny Tales," for example, contains stories as brief as one minute. The "Riddle Tales" and "Participation Tales" can be as long or as short as you like, depending on how much time you want to give the audience to contribute answers or how you want to extend the participation sequences.

I have gathered many of these stories from friends as I travel. At a *supra* banquet in Tbilisi, Georgia, the guests peppered me with Georgian tales and instructed me to pass them on to the world. The Georgians insist that wine originated in their beautiful country . . . and wanted me to tell "Wine Is Born in Georgia" to prove it. My Basque hosts at the American International School in Bilbao brought out a collection of Basque tales they thought I should share. Masako Sueyoshi, who takes me on wonderful storytelling tours in Japan, told me her delightful version of "The Mouse Sutra." Wajuppa Tossa, my host when I was a Fulbright Scholar in Mahasarakham, Thailand, just keeps coming up with more and more delightful Thai/Lao folktales. Livia de Almeida from Rio de Janeiro and Murti Bunanta of Jakarta both have worked with me on collections of tales from their countries, and some of these tales deserved a somewhat briefer retelling in this book. "Coyote Steals a Bag" I learned from a librarian in Caspar, Wyoming. I was told "Swimming to Kotzebue" by the Eskimo elder Lela Kiana Oman while interviewing her for my book *Ten Traditional Tellers* (Bloomington: University of Illinois Press, 2006). And some of the tales, such as Naomi Baltuck's "What Herschel's Father Did" and "The Douglas Fir Cone"—which I learned from a park naturalist—I learned in my own hometown of Seattle. Some of these tales I learned third-hand; for example, at a workshop in Mahasarakham, Thailand, JonLee Joseph, who had just returned from two years of teaching in China, told me a poignant tale she heard there, which is included here as "The Papercut Woman."

Thus stories emerge and merge and travel . . . from next door or around the world. I hope you will take some of these stories—whichever delight you most—and move them on their way. Pass them to another teller . . . and another . . .

—MRM

ABOUT THE TALE NOTES

In the notes following the tales, I give references to folktale motif-indexes that have included these stories. The sources I refer to are:

Aarne, Antti and Stith Thompson. *The Types of the Folktale.* Helsinki: Folklore Fellows Communication, 1961.

MacDonald, Margaret Read. *The Storyteller's Sourcebook: A Subject, Title, and Motif-Index to Folklore Collections for Children.* lst edition. Detroit: Neal–Schuman/Gale Research, 1982.

MacDonald, Margaret Read and Brian W. Sturm. *The Storyteller's Sourcebook: A Subject, Title, and Motif-Index to Folklore Collections for Children: 1983–1999.* Farmington Hills, Michigan: Gale Group, 2000.

Thompson, Stith. *Motif-Index of Folk-Literature.* 6 vols. Bloomington: Indiana University Press, 1966.

You may consult those indexes as well as the sources cited in the tale notes to find more variants of the stories shared here.

Participation Tales

You can make these stories as wild or as quiet as you like. They make good "stretches" between stories. You can ask the audience to stand as you tell these tales and mime the action with you. When telling "Monkeys in the Rain" and "Take a Little Walk, Bear," I ask my listeners to repeat everything I say.

I learned "Take a Little Walk, Bear" from Mary Banbury, a Seattle-area teacher. She couldn't recall where she had learned it. Just yesterday I met another teacher who has told the story since the 1980s. She couldn't recall where she had learned it, either. And her version was different from Mary's . . . and from mine. The story is clearly a take-off on the folktale "Going on a Bear Hunt." I've included a camp version of that tale here, as told by Hong Kong International School teacher and storyteller Nat Whitman.

"In a Dark, Dark House" is a favorite scary tale for young listeners among librarians and teachers. But I hadn't heard it told as a participation tale until I saw Jeffrey Brewster doing it with the kindergartners at the International School of Brussels.

"Monkeys in the Rain" and "Two Frogs in a Cream Jar" grew out of my tellings in Indonesia in rural areas where no one spoke English. Lots of movement was needed!

"Phya Khankhaak" is the most difficult story of this set. But it does make for great participation if you invite all of the children to choose the part of an animal and grunt, growl, or howl as you climb to the heavens to demand rain of the Sky God, Phya Thaen. This tale, known to every child in Laos and Northeastern Thailand, explains the annual Bun Bang Fai festival during which rockets are shot into the sky—to remind Phya Thaen to send rain, of course!

Monkeys in the Rain
A Folktale from Brazil

 3 minutes

■ The audience should echo everything the teller says
beginning with line three.

Five little monkeys lived in a tree.
When they woke up, the sun was shining!

■ Tell the audience to say everything you say and do everything you do.

"The sun is shining!   Make sun over head with arms.
Let's play!"   Act out swinging through the trees;
                              repeat several times.

Hand-over-hand-over hand . . ."It's fun!"
Hand-over-hand-over hand . . ."It's fun!"

■ Pause. Then . . .

"Let's play tag!"

■ Suggest that listeners tag one person to their right,
then one person on their left . . . gently.

"Oo-oo-oo-oo-oo-oo"   Swinging and calling
"Caught you!"   Reach out as if to touch another monkey.
"Oo-oo-oo-oo-oo-oo"   Swinging and calling
"Caught you!"   Reach out.

■ Slap legs to simulate rain.

"Rain! Rain! Rain! RAIN!"

"I'm cold!"
"I'm wet!"
"We should build a house!"
"Let's build a house."

Pause to encourage audience to chant after you.

■ Pause as if thinking about this.

"Tomorrow!"
"Tomorrow?"
"Tomorrow!"

Next day . . .
The sun was shining!
"Let's play!"
Hand-over-hand-over hand . . ."It's fun!"
Hand-over-hand-over hand . . ."It's fun!"

"Let's play tag!"
"Oo-oo-oo-oo-oo-oo"
"Caught you!"
"Oo-oo-oo-oo-oo-oo"
"Caught you!"

"Rain! Rain! Rain! RAIN!"

"I'm cold!"
"I'm wet!"
"We should build a house!"
"Let's build a house!"
"Tomorrow."
"Tomorrow?"
"Tomorrow."

Next day . . .
The sun was shining!
"Let's play!"
Hand-over-hand-over hand . . ."It's fun!"
Hand-over-hand-over hand . . ."It's fun!"

"Let's play tag!"
"Oo-oo-oo-oo-oo-oo"
"Caught you!"
"Oo-oo-oo-oo-oo-oo"
"Caught you!"

"Rain! Rain! Rain! RAIN!"

"I'm cold!"
"I'm wet!"
"We should build a house!"
"Let's build a house!"
"Tomorrow."
"Tomorrow?"
"Tomorrow."

> Keep questioning the idea of "Tomorrow?" until someone in the audience says, "Today!" Acknowledge the answer and deliver the final sentence, without the audience's repetition.

Don't be like the monkeys.
Do it ... TODAY!

Retold from "The Monkey's House" in *Valery Carrick's Tales of Wise and Foolish Animals* by Valery Carrick (New York: Dover, 1969), pp. 91–95. Originally published by Frederick Stokes, 1928. A Brazilian version appears in Moritz Jagendorf and Ralph Steele Boggs, *King of the Mountain* (New York: Vanguard, 1960). For a delightful picture book of this tale see *So Say the Little Monkeys* by Nancy Van Laan (New York: Atheneum, 1998). J2171.2.1 *Does not need roof when it is fair; cannot put it on when it rains.* Stith Thompson cites variants from Italy, Japan, Russia, and Aesop. Related also to A2233.2.1 *Too cold for hare (dog) to build house in winter, not necessary in summer.* I usually let the audience members reach out and tag each other when the monkeys play tag. If your audience is rousty, tell them that they can each just tag one person on the right and one on the left during the tag session. I say: "Tag ... RIGHT ... Tag ... LEFT ... STOP!" You can usually bring the audience back to attention by patting your knees and calling "Rain ... rain ... rain ..." for quite a while. Or if they are *really* insane ... I just leave out the tagging part.

Take a Little Walk, Bear

Teacher Lore

 5 minutes, depending on how much time you take with the actions

Little Bear wanted to go out and see the world.
"You may go out, Little Bear," said his Momma.
"But pay attention to what I tell you now:
STAY AWAY FROM THE BEES."

"Oh yes, Momma.
I'll stay away from the bees."

So Little Bear went out the door.
The world looked big and wonderful!
"Ohhhhh!"

> Slap legs as you "walk."

"Take a little walk, Bear,
walk, Bear,
walk, Bear.
Take a little walk, Bear,
walk, Bear,
walk."

> Repeat this and each subsequent refrain three times and make the
> motions to accompany the rhyme.

Suddenly . . . BZZZZZZ
there was a . . . BEE!

"BEES!
BEES mean HONEY!"

18

Little Bear forgot what his Momma had told him.
He started following that bee.

▌ Walk faster now . . .

"Take a little walk, Bear,
walk, Bear,
walk, Bear.
Take a little walk, Bear,
walk, Bear,
walk."

The bee flew over a stream.
Little Bear waded right in.

▌ Lift your feet up high to wade.

"Take a little wade, Bear,
wade, Bear,
wade, Bear.
Take a little wade, Bear,
wade, Bear,
wade."

The bee flew over a meadow.
Little Bear went right after it.

"Take a little skip, Bear,
skip, Bear,
skip, Bear.
Take a little skip, Bear,
skip, Bear,
skip."

The bee flew into a hole in the top of a big tree!

"Take a little climb, Bear,
climb, Bear,

climb, Bear.
Take a little climb, Bear,
climb, Bear,
climb."

Little Bear smelled something.

"Take a little smell, Bear,
smell, Bear,
smell, Bear.
Take a little smell, Bear,
smell, Bear,
smell."

"It smells like honey!"

"Take a little look, Bear,
look, Bear,
look, Bear.
Take a little look, Bear,
look, Bear,
look."

"It *looks* like honey!"

"Take a little taste, Bear,
taste, Bear,
taste, Bear.
Take a little taste, Bear,
taste, Bear,
taste."

"It IS honey!
YOW! BEEES!
I want my MOMMA!"

■ Repeat everything rapidly, in reverse sequence from "climb"

"Take a little climb, Bear, climb, Bear, climb, Bear . . .
Take a little skip, Bear, skip, Bear, skip, Bear . . .
Take a little wade, Bear, wade, Bear, wade, Bear . . .
Take a little walk, Bear, walk, Bear, walk, Bear—"

"MOMMA! MOMMA! BEES STUNG ME!!!"

"Well then . . .
Take a little hug, Bear,
hug, Bear,
hug, Bear.
Take a little hug, Bear,
hug, Bear,
HUG."

I learned this tale several years ago from Mary Branbury, a Seattle
preschool teacher. Mary had learned it years before from another
teacher. I recently heard a different version from Roxanne Garzon,
another Seattle worker with young children. Roxanne says she learned
it years ago from another teacher too. Their versions are slightly different
from each other. And my own version has developed over the years to
differ from both of theirs. Clearly some teacher once took the traditional chant "Going on a Bear Hunt" (an old camp favorite; see next
selection) and tailored it especially for young listeners to create this new
version—and everyone who tells it changes it a little bit more. This is a
perfect example of the folklore process at work. Add in whatever you
want—a field of grass *(swish swish),* a puddle of mud *(squish squish),* etc.
It is nice to end the story by having the children put their arms around
themselves and give themselves a Mother Bear hug. Or if the group is
small enough, you can give them all a bear hug yourself!

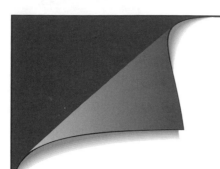

Going on a Bear Hunt

An American Folk Chant
as told by Nat Whitman

5 minutes or more, depending on how rapidly you tell and how many extensions you insert

Audience repeats everything the leader says and does.
Leader slaps sides of thighs in sweeping-down motion on every downbeat, brings hands up to a clap in front of him on every upbeat.
He keeps this up throughout chant and until he sees the next obstacle.

LEADER	GROUP
Going on a bear hunt!	Going on a bear hunt!
I'm not afraid!	I'm not afraid!
I've got my pack on my back.	I've got my pack on my back.
And twenty bullets in my sack.	And twenty bullets in my sack.

Continue clapping and slapping for a few times, stopping on next line

Oh, STOP!	Oh, STOP!
There's a river!	There's a river!
Can't go around it!	Can't go around it!
Can't go under it!	Can't go under it!
Have to swim THROUGH it!	Have to swim THROUGH it!

All right.	All right.
Let's go.	Let's go.
Splash! Splash! Swish! Swish!	*Splash! Splash! Swish! Swish!*

Make swimming motions and sounds, inviting audience to join you.

Going on a bear hunt!	Going on a bear hunt!

Action repeats over and over. Add whatever obstacles you think of—a swamp, a field, a rock, a tree, etc. Use the phrases "Can't go around it . . . Can't go under it . . ." The final obstacle you reach is a cave.

Oh, STOP!
There's a cave!
Can't go around it.
Can't go under it.
Better go in it.

Okay.
Let's go.

▌ Tiptoe nervously.

Uh, oh.
I feel something.
It feels like a big, furry dog.
I smell something.
It smells like a big furry dog.
Get my matches.
Strike a light.
It's a BEAR!
Let's get out of here!

Oh, STOP!
There's a cave!
Can't go around it.
Can't go under it.
Better go in it.

Okay.
Let's go.

Uh, oh.
I feel something.
It feels like a big, furry dog.
I smell something.
It smells like a big furry dog.
Get my matches.
Strike a light.
It's a BEAR!
Let's get out of here!

▌ Do the return chants as fast as possible, all together, audience and leader.

Going on a bear hunt!
I'm not afraid!
I've got my pack on my back.
And twenty bullets in my sack.

Going on a bear hunt!
I'm not afraid!
I've got my pack on my back.
And twenty bullets in my sack.

▌ Climb, swim, or pass every obstacle in reverse order as you race back, repeating the entire chant as fast as you can as you mime negotiating each obstacle.

In the house!
Close the door!

In the house!
Close the door!

▌ Relaxing, coolly.

But I wasn't afraid!

But I wasn't afraid!

As told by Nat Whitman in Ban Kruat, Thailand New Year's Eve, 1996. Nat learned this at Bear-Pole Ranch, near Steamboat Springs, Colorado, circa 1986. For another version see "Let's Go on a Bear Hunt" in *A Parent's Guide to Storytelling* by Margaret Read MacDonald (Little Rock: August House, 1995). MacDonald learned this circa 1952 at a family reunion in southern Indiana.

In a Dark, Dark House

An American Folktale
as told by Jeffrey Brewster

1 minute, or slightly longer, depending on elaboration

In a dark, dark forest . . .	Form tree with right hand cupping left elbow and wriggle fingers like leaves.
there was a dark, dark house.	Form large house shape with hands over head.
In that dark, dark house . . .	
there was a dark, dark room.	Smaller shape with hands.
In that dark, dark room . . .	
there was a dark, dark cupboard.	Mime opening cupboard.
In that dark, dark cupboard . . .	
there was a dark, dark box	Form small box shape with hand.
AND in the dark, dark box . . .	
There was . . .	Mime opening box . . . slowly.
NOTHING!	Or say "A GHOST!" if you prefer.

I first saw this fingerplay adaptation of the classic tale led very deliberately and slowly with preschoolers by Jeffrey Brewster, school librarian at the International School of Brussels. Thanks to Jeffrey for permission to share. Z13.1 *Tale-teller frightens listener: yells "Boo" at exciting point.* MacDonald Z13.1.4 ★ *Person enters dark, dark house. . . .*

Two Frogs in a Cream Jar

A Russian Fable inspired by
Martha Hamilton and Mitch Weiss

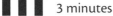 3 minutes

Divide audience into two groups. One takes the role of each frog. Ask them to repeat your words and actions.

Two frogs fell into a jar of cream.	Splash fists down and open.
#1: "Swim!"	Direct Group One to say this and make paddling motion with hands.
#2: "I'm swimming!"	Direct Group Two to say this and make paddling motion.
#1: "Swim!"	Side One: paddling
#2: "I'm swimming!"	Side Two: paddling
#1: "Swim!"	Side One: paddling
#2: "I'm swimming!"	Side Two: paddling
#1: "Don't give up!"	Side One: getting tired but still paddling
#2: "I won't give up!"	Side Two: getting tired but still paddling
#1: Don't give up!"	Side One: very tired but still paddling
#2: "I want to give up."	Side Two: paddling weekly but starting to fail
#1: "Don't give up!"	Side One: very tired but still . . . paddling

25

#2: "I'm going to give up . . . glub . . . glub . . . glub . . ."

Side Two: arms up as if sinking

#1: "Never give up!
Never give up!
Never give up!
Never give up!
Never . . . what?

Side One: still paddling

Reach down with feet as if touching solid ground.

What's this?
I can stand up!
How is this possible?"

Stop paddling and hop around.

▌ Let audience answer the riddle.

Yes!
And the moral is . . .

NEVER GIVE UP!

I was inspired to start telling this after a conversation with Martha Hamilton, who, with her husband and storytelling partner, Mitch Weiss, was preparing a version for publication in *A Tale of Two Frogs* (Atlanta: August House Story Cove, 2006). MacDonald Q81.2★ *Reward for perseverance. Two frogs in crock of cream. One drowns. Second kicks until cream turns to butter. Escapes.* MacDonald cites three Russian variants and one Aesop. Another fun tale is found in Ellis Credle, *Tall Tales from the High Hills* (New York: Nelson, 1957). pp. 89–95. MacDonald J1689.2★ *College educated son has father put frogs in churn to churn butter, invents self-kicking machine.*

Phya Khankhaak, the Toad Prince

A Lao Folktale from Isaan (Northeastern Thailand) as told by Wajuppa Tossa

 5 minutes

When Phya Khankhaak was born,
his mother was the queen
and his father was the king.
But the baby looked just like a toad!
Of course no one said anything about the way he looked.

Still, everyone called him "Khankhaak,"
which means "toad." It even *sounds* like a toad.
"Khan KHAAK!"

And as he grew, he continued to look more and more like a . . . toad.
He was a little toad boy.
Then he was a little toad teenager.

By the time Khankhaak was twenty, he was tired of looking like a toad.

He told his father that he wanted a palace of his own.
He wanted a palace with one thousand rooms and ten thousand pillars . . .
and a jeweled roof.
And he wanted a beautiful wife too!

His father said, "Impossible!"

But one of the gods, Indra, liked Khankhaak.
Indra created a palace with one thousand rooms, ten thousand pillars . . .
and a jeweled roof.

There was even a beautiful young lady in the palace!

When Khankhaak saw all this, he was delighted.
"YES!" And he quickly peeled off his toad-form!
It came off just like a suit of clothes.
And there stood Khankhaak, as handsome as a god!

Now he was called Phya Khankhaak, LORD Khankhaak.
He was so popular that everyone came to his palace.
Soon no one was paying attention to Phya Thaen, the god of the heavens.

Phya Thaen became angrier and angrier.
At last he took action.
Phya Thaen forbade the nagas to swim anymore in his golden pond.
The nagas were giant magical snakes.
Whenever the nagas swam, they flipped their tails and splashed water out of the pond.
This water fell to the earth as rain.
If the nagas could not swim . . .
No rain ever fell on the earth below.

Soon people were suffering.
Their crops withered, their streams dried up.

When Khankhaak saw this,
he called together a large army to march to heaven.
They would demand that Phya Thaen let rain fall.

Not only humans joined the march,
but all of the animals came too.
The animals were suffering very much without rain.

Which animals do you think might have come along?

> As listeners suggest animals, ask them what noise that animal makes. Ask
> for volunteers to help make that animal sound. Make sure everyone has a
> part, then continue the story.

Off they marched to heaven.
They were chanting:

> Phya Thaen!
> Give us rain!
>
> Phya Thaen!
> Give us rain!

Phya Thaen heard them coming.
Their chants frightened him.
"Maybe I should let them have their rain."

When they reached his palace, they halted.
Then all together they let out their most ferocious roar!

> Cue listeners to all make their animal sounds as loudly as possible on the count of three.

Phya Thaen was terrified!
"OK! OK! You may have your water!"

Phya Thaen sent the nagas into Golden Pond at once.
They began to swim around and swish their tails.
Soon water began to splash over the edge of the pond.
And the cool water began to fall to the earth.

So Phya Khankhaak led his great army back down to earth.
But before he left the heavens, he made Phya Thaen promise
NEVER to stop the rains again.

Phya Thaen promised.

But Phya Thaen might forget.
So every year, the Lao people shoot rockets into the sky just to remind him.

Phya Thaen!
Give us RAIN!

Phya Thaen!
Give us RAIN!

And usually . . . the rain falls.

Retold from *Phya Khankhaak, the Toad King* by Wajuppa
Tossa (Lewisburg, Pennsylvania: Bucknell University
Press, 1996). Inspired also by performances of Dr.
Wajuppa and her Mahasarakham Storytelling Troupe.
This mythology is tied to Bun Bang Fai, the rocket fes-
tival of Isaan, and explains the gigantic rockets that are
fired into the air each spring. The custom takes place in
Isaan, a Lao cultural area of Northeastern Thailand, as
well as in the country of Laos.

Animal Tales

You will notice that the animals in our "Animal Tales" all act a great deal like humans. An "animal" story is often a gentle way to remind folks of the ways we humans should—or should not—behave.

It could be interesting to share the animal story "Human's Age" alongside the origin story "Wine Is Born in Georgia" (which could just as easily have been placed in this section). Both compare man's characteristics to those of animals.

I include three versions of "Christmas of the Animals." It is interested to see how a simple folk tradition becomes elaborated into a story in the hands of a master teller such as Joe Hayes. This is a useful traditional tale to add to your Christmas or Festival of Lights repertoire.

Coyote Steals a Bag
A Maidu Folktale

 3 minutes, 30 second

Coyote was going there, going there, going there . . .
He heard a sound!
Scrabble . . . scrabble . . . thunk!
Scrabble . . . scrabble . . . thunk!

There was Mole.
Mole was shoveling dirt out of his hole.
Scrabble . . . scrabble . . . thunk!
Scrabble . . . scrabble . . . thunk!

"Hey, Mole!" called Coyote.

WHUNK! Mole disappeared down his hole.
Coyote sat down and waited for Mole to come up again.

Scrabble . . . scrabble . . . thunk!
Mole shoved out a pile of dirt.
"How are you today, Mole?"

WHUNK! Mole disappeared down his hole.
"Not very talkative," thought Coyote.

Next time Mole came up, Coyote was very close to his hole.
"Hi, MOLE!"

"Hi, Coyote!"
WHUNK! Mole was gone again.

But Coyote had noticed something strange on Mole's back.
There was a large bag hanging there . . . right on Mole's back.
It seemed to be full of something.

Scrabble . . . scrabble . . . thunk!
Up came Mole.
"Hey, Mole . . . what's in your bag?"
"None of your business."
WHUNK!

Now Coyote was interested.
What could Mole have in his bag?
Maybe something good to eat.
Maybe money.
Maybe . . .
Coyote had to find out.

Scrabble . . . scrabble . . . thunk!

"Looks like it's full," said Coyote. "What's in it, anyway?"
"Won't tell you," Mole replied.
WHUNK!

Coyote couldn't stand this.
He got really close to Mole's hole.
He reached out his paw. . . .

Scrabble . . . scrabble . . . thunk!
Up came Mole.

Coyote GRABBED that bag and snatched it off Mole's back.
"Got it now!"

"Just KEEP it, Coyote!"
WHUNK!
Mole was gone.
Coyote was delighted!

"A whole bag of goodies—just for ME!"
Coyote ran behind the big rock and started pawing at the bag's drawstring.
It was tied tight.
Coyote shook the bag . . . couldn't tell what it was.
He smelled the bag . . . couldn't tell what it was.
He poked a little hole in the bag and peered in . . . couldn't see anything.
So he just RIPPED the bag open.

Zzzzzzzzzz . . . . .out came a black, whirring cloud!
That cloud whirred around and began to settle all over Coyote.
Suddenly he felt something.
"YOW!" It was a little bite!
"YOW! YOW! YOW!" LOTS of little bites.
Coyote was covered with . . . FLEAS!!!

"Fleas! Fleas! Fleas!
Off! Off! Off!!"

But no matter how Coyote scratched and pawed at himself
those fleas did not get off.
They had found a good old wooly hide, and they liked it!

"Better even than MOLE!" they whispered.
"We're going to live right here FOREVER!"

And so they do.
Watch Coyote. You will see him scratch and scratch.
But those fleas just stay right with him.
After all . . . he's the one that stole them!

I heard this story from Glenda Williams at the Natrona County
Public Library in Caspar, Wyoming, on January 11, 2006. Glenda
had elaborated on a tale in *Meet Tricky Coyote!* by Gretchen Will
Mayo (New York: Walker & Co., 1993), pp. 11–14. According to
Mayo's notes, the story was collected in 1899 from a Maidu teller.
This reminds of the many tales of foolish encounters with wasp
nests cited in K1023 *Getting honey from the wasp-nest. The dupe is
stung.* Type 49.

Cricket and Jaguar Fight

A Mayan Folktale from Zinacantán,
Chiapas, Mexico

 4 minutes

Cricket was very tiny.
He always walked bent over with his face to the ground,
and he hardly ever spoke to anyone.

One day Jaguar came striding down the path, and CRUNCH . . .
He stepped right on Cricket.

"Hey! Don't you have eyes in your head?" called Cricket.
"You just stepped on me!
That hurts!"

"Big deal," answered Jaguar.
"This is my path.
I can stomp on anything that gets in my way."

"This is not your path.
This path belongs to everybody.
Who do you think you are to be such a big bully?
How strong do you think you are, anyway?"

"I'm a lot stronger than you, Cricket.
You are too tiny to count for anything."

Cricket was really fuming.
"You think you are so strong!
How about a contest?
Let's do battle and see who is the strongest."

Jaguar couldn't believe that the tiny cricket would challenge him.
But Cricket kept pushing . . .
So finally Jaguar said,

"Meet me here tomorrow.
I'll bring my army.
You can bring yours.
We'll see who is stronger, little Cricket!"

When Jaguar arrived he was leading an army of huge snakes.

"Our turn first!" said Jaguar.
"Army . . . attack Cricket!"

The snakes came right at Cricket.
But when the first snake lunged at him . . .
He simply *jumped* into the air.

A second snake came striking with open fangs.
But Cricket . . . *jumped!*

Another snake rushed in. No use!
Cricket saw him coming and . . . *jumped!*

Jaguar was furious.
"Catch that cricket!
Bite him!"

"He is too quick," hissed the snakes.
"He jumps before we can strike."

"Then wrap yourselves around him and squeeze him to death!"

"How can we wrap ourselves around something so tiny?
It is impossible."

At last Jaguar had to admit that his army had failed to bring down the cricket.

"Now it's turn for *my* army!" cried Cricket.
He gave a sharp little whistle.
Suddenly the earth was swarming with *insects!*
Bees, yellow wasps, black wasps, hornets . . .
Everything that stings came flying right at Jaguar.

"ROAAWWRR!" Jaguar turned tail and ran.
His snake army slithered after him.
There was no way they could stand up and fight against this army of stinging insects.

"Thank you for defending me!" Cricket called to his army.
"We won!
From now on, no one will pester us.
Go and build your nests wherever you want.
Hang them in hollow trees,
put them where you like.
Hang there and be happy!
No one will squash us now."

"This is good," said the insects to each other.
"This is good."

"But as for me," said little Cricket,
"I am not going to talk anymore.
When I talk I just into trouble.
From now on, I will just *sing.*"

And so he does.
Every night you will hear cricket's song—
"*Cheel cheel cheel!*"
That's the only voice he has now.

So the world was left in good shape.
Unless a wasp gets you!

Retold from "War between the Cricket and the
Jaguar" in *The People of the Bat: Mayan Tales and
Dreams from Zinacantán* by Robert M. Laughlin
(Washington, D.C.: Smithsonian Institution, 1988).
The story was told by Petul Vaskis. Laughlin's book
contains stories from the Tzotzil-speaking Maya
of Zinacantán, a community in the highlands of
Chiapas, Mexico. Retold with permission of
Robert M. Laughlin. A donation will be made to
the Sna Jtz'ibajom project in the name of the teller,
Petul Vaskis. For another version of this tale see
MacDonald B263.9★ *War between insects and animals.
Insects cloud sun and sting animals in dark. Cricket and
lion start feud.* See also Stith Thompson B263.2 *War
between elephants and ants* for an Indonesian variant.
And B268.8.1 *Army of hornets* with Jewish variants.
Under L315.6 *Insects worry large animal to despair or
death.* Thompson cites variants from Spain, Japan, and
Indonesia. A French version is cited in MacDonald
and Sturm B263.9.1★ *Bear and beetle declare war, gather
armies. Bear gets large mammals, while beetle gets hornets
and insects. Small insects sting large.*

One Night's Sleep

A Coast Salish Folktale

1 minute, 30 seconds

Frog and Bear were trying to decide how long they should sleep.

"Let us sleep four or five years," said Bear.
But Frog began to argue in little frog-talk.

"One night! One night! One night!" called Frog.
"Five years. Five years," insisted Bear.

"One night! One night! One night!"
"Four years. Four years."

"One night! One night! One night!"
"Three years. Three years."

"One night! One night! One night!"
"Two years. Two years."

"One night! One night! One night!"
"One year. One year." Bear was giving up.

Frog stopped.

All of Frog's friends jumped out of the pond and lined up.
"One year? One year? One year?"
The frogs all bobbed up and down, considering this.
"One year. One year. One year," the frogs agreed.

"All right," said Bear.
"I one year. You one year."

The frogs all began to croak in their little frog voices, "OK! OK! OK!
Frogs one year.
Bear one year.
But people . . . just sleep . . . ONE NIGHT!"

So that's the way it was decided.

Bear sleeps all winter.
In February he puts out his paw. Too cold.
In March he puts out his paw. Still too cold.
In April he puts out his paw. Warm enough.
And Bear gets up.

Frog sleeps all winter too.
In November his mud freezes.
But in April his mud thaws.
And Frog gets up.

But as for humans . . . we get to sleep . . . just one night.

Retold from *Folk-tales of the Coast Salish,* collected
and edited by Thelma Adamson (New York: The
American Folk-Lore Society/G.E. Stechert and Co.,
1934), pp. 189–190. This tale was collected in 1926
from Mary Iley, who used hand motions as she told
the story, holding her fingers up when the frogs
popped up and bending them down when the frogs
popped back down again. A similar story, told by Lucy
Youckton in 1926, is on pp. 188–189 in the same
book. In that story, Bear argues with Big Yellowjacket,
Black Yellowjacket, Frog, and Grouse. Johnny Moses
tells a delightful version of this story featuring Bear
and Ant. You can hear it on his audio CD, *American
Indian Voices* (available at www.johnnymoses.com).
A1172 *Determination of night and day. After much discus-
sion, the relative length of these divisions is determined.*
A1399.2.1 *Origin of sleep.*

Christmas of the Animals

Based on an Original Story by Joe Hayes
incorporating New Mexican Folk Traditions
(copyright © 1989)

■▪ 1 minute, 30 seconds

In New Mexico there was once a little village so remote that the people had little contact with the rest of the world. They depended on the wood-cutter Teófilo to let them know when important dates like Christmas were coming round. Then people would get out their *nacimiento*—manger scenes—and put out their *luminarios*—lights.

Teófilo kept the days of the year marked on his wall. So he always knew what day it was. But this year he was so busy that he forgot to tell anyone that it was time for Christmas.

Teófilo's old donkey was very upset about this. After all, the donkey had a very important role in the Christmas story, no? The days went by and still the people did nothing to prepare for La Noche Buena. So the donkey called a meeting of all the animals.

"The people have forgotten to prepare for La Noche Buena," complained the donkey.
"This is not right."

But the rooster had an idea. "I've been thinking about this, and I have a plan. I have written a Christmas play for us. You all go home and practice your parts. When I give the signal, everyone speak your lines."

Christmas Eve came, and still the people had done nothing. The children were all asleep in their beds when suddenly they were awakened by the rooster crowing from the top of the church.

"¡Cristo nació! ¡Cristo nació!"

Down below, the old donkey called out his part, *"¿Dónde? ¿Dónde?"*
And the sheep answered, *"En Belén. En Belén."*
Then all of the little chicks began to cluck, *"¿Pa' qué? ¿Pa' qué?"*
And the cow answered, *"¡Amor! ¡Amor!"*
While the ducks quacked, *"¡Paz! ¡Paz!"*

The children shook their parents awake.
"Listen! Listen!
'¡Cristo es nació!' That means Christ is born!
'¿Dónde?' Where?
'En Belén.' In Bethlehem.
'¿Pa' qué?' Why?
'Amour' is Love,
and *'Paz'* is "Peace."

Then everyone jumped out of bed, set out their *nacimiento,* put out their *luminarios,* and hurried off to church for the Midnight Mass. Ever since then this has been called the Misa del Gallo—the Mass of the Cock.

I don't think that was fair, do you? After all, who was it that remembered La Noche Buena? Who do you think should get the credit? I think it should be the old donkey. I complained to Teófilo about this, and do you know what he said?

"Look at your donkey. Down his back there is a row of black hairs. And across his shoulders there is another row. That makes the sign of the cross. The donkey is marked forever. He has his reward. If you don't believe me, when you get home tonight go check your donkey. You will see I'm telling you the truth."

Maggie Bennett told this at the 2002 Christmas program of the Seattle Storyteller's Guild. The tale could be told either with or without the last two paragraphs. It was written by Joe Hayes, a New Mexican storyteller. Joe says he created the story from several New Mexican folk motifs. By placing the talking-animal tradition within the frame story of the woodcutter's family, he creates a delightful tale. Joe has graciously given permission for its use here. He points out that the woodcutter's name is Teófilo, not Tío, and that the tale is his creation except for the animal's speeches on Christmas Eve. The story was published as *The Wise Little Burro* by Joe Hayes (Santa Fe: Trails West Publishing, 1989). Motif B251.1.2 *Animals speak to one another at Christmas.* Stith Thompson cites sources from Germany, Brittany, Lithuania, Livonia, and North Carolina. He cites Child ballads under B251.2.1 *Cock crows, "Christus natus est."* Baughman cites a related tradition, B251.1.2.3 *Cows kneel in stable at midnight of Eve of Old Christmas.* He found sources from Hereford, Cornwall, Masssachussets, South Carolina (African-American), and Missouri. In another tale of animals talking on Christmas Eve, brothers vie to hear the animals tell where treasure is buried (Katherine Briggs, *Folktales of England,* (Chicago: University of Chicago Press, 1965), pp. 44–46).

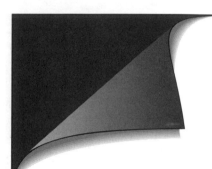

Christmas of the Animals, *Version Two*
Mexican Folk Tradition

▮ 45 seconds

It is said that when Christ was born, the cock crowed,
"¡Cristo nació! ¡Cristo nació!"
("Christ is born!")

Somebody called, "Where?"

So the little bearded billy goat answered,
"¡En Beléeeeeen!" "¡En Beléeeeeen!"
("In Bethlehem!")

Then the billy goat became so excited that he began to jump for joy . . .
and *oops!* He fell into the well!
Everyone heard his cries for help and hurried to the well.

The dove saw him struggling in the water down there and cooed out,
"¡Por pendejo se cayó!" "¡Por pendejo se cayó!
(Because he's a fool, he fell!)

And the turkeys rushed around trying to help by calling:
"¡Cien dólares al que lo saque!" "¡Cien dólares al que lo saque!"
(A hundred dollars to whomever gets him out!)

Retold from "Talking Animals" in *Folktales of Mexico*
by Américo Paredes (Chicago: University of Chicago,
1970), p.194. Collected in 1962 from J.F., a mestizo
man in his fifties, in Ajusco, Mexico. B251.2.1 *Cock
crows, "Christus natus est."* B251.1.2 *Animals speak to
one another at Christmas.*

Christmas of the Animals, *Version Three*

Hispanic tradition, Brownsville, Texas

■ 15 seconds

When Christ was born, the cock began to crow,
"¡Cristo nació! ¡Cristo nació!" (Christ is born!)

And the sheep added,
"¡En Belén! ¡En Belén!" (In Bethelehem!)

While the fat turkey excitedly shouted out,
"¡Gordo! ¡Gordo! ¡Gordo! ¡Gordo!" (Fat, fat, fat, fat baby!)

Retold from "Talking Animals" in *Folktales of Mexico*
by Américo Paredes (Chicago: University of Chicago,
1970), p. 237. Recalled from Paredes' childhood.
B251.2.1 *Cock crows, "Christus natus est."* B251.1.2
Animals speak to one another at Christmas.

Human's Age
A Folktale from Laos
Retold by Wajuppa Tossa

 4 minutes, 30 seconds

Once long ago, after the world was newly created, Phya Thaen, the highest god in Lao tradition, realized that he had not given an age limit to humans or to some of the animals. So he called Man, Buffalo, Dog, and Monkey to a meeting in heaven.

Once they were there, he said, "Now, as I have not given you your ages, I would like to do so today."

"Yes, My Lord," said all the creatures in unison.

"Man, your age limit on earth is thirty," said Phya Thaen.

"Oh, thank you, My Lord," said Man.

"Buffalo, Dog, and Monkey, I want you to be here to help man. So I am giving you each thirty years as well. Buffalo, it will be your job to work hard for Man and plow his fields. You can do this for the thirty years that Man lives. So I give you thirty years."

"Oh, thank you kindly, Your Majesty, but I would rather stay for only ten years on earth. If I have to work so hard, I think ten years is enough. That's plenty for me," said Buffalo.

"Granted," said Phya Thaen.

Man was listening to all this. The nature of the human is greediness. Thus he saw his chance of gaining more time on earth.

"Your Majesty, if Buffalo does not want to use his quota of time on earth, I would like to have the number of years that he does not want," said Man.

"Granted," said Phya Thaen. "Now, let's look at Dog. You were born to be on guard during the night when the humans are sleeping. You will be forever awake during the night. I will give you thirty years as well," said Phya Thaen.

"Your Majesty, if I have to stay awake all night every night, I think ten years is plenty. Could you please just give me only ten years?"

"Granted," said Phya Thaen.

Again, the human's greed overtook him, so he said, "Your Majesty, if the dog does not want to use his quota of time on earth, I would like to have the number of years that he does not want."

"Granted," said Phya Thaen. "Now, let's consider Monkey's age. I sent you to be born on earth to entertain the humans after their hard work. You must be able to make them laugh. I give you also thirty years," said Phya Thaen.

"Oh, Your Majesty, I don't know if I can be funny for thirty years. It might be difficult to make humans laugh. Could I just have ten years, please?"

Again Man's greed took control over him. "Your Majesty, if Monkey does not want to use his quota of time on earth, I would like to have the number of years to add to my original age."

"Granted," said Phya Thaen.

Phya Thaen then made his final proclamation: "From now on, Buffalo will have ten years on earth. Dog will have ten years on earth. Monkey will have ten years on earth. Man will have his original thirty. But he can also have twenty years from Buffalo, twenty from Dog, and twenty from Monkey."

And so it is.

But the Lao people have noticed that Man only behaves like a human in those first thirty years of his life. These were the years Phya Thaen originally gave to Man. Between the ages of thirty and fifty, Man behaves like Buffalo. He works very hard all the time. Between the age of fifty and seventy, Man uses up the years he borrowed from Dog. Now he cannot sleep at all. He stays awake all night worrying. But finally he reaches the years between seventy and ninety, the years he borrowed from Monkey. And then Man just wanders about doing foolish things and making people laugh.

Told by Pha Sunantha Theerapanyophikkhu, Vientiane, Laos. Retold from *Lao Tales* by Wajuppa Tossa and Kongdeuanne Nettavong (Westport, Connecticut: Libraries Unlimited, 2007). A1321 *Men and animals readjust span of life*. Stith Thompson's *Motif-Index of Folk-Literature* cites variants of this story from Lithuania, Turkey, India, and an Aesop version. B592 *Animals bequeath characteristics to man*. Wajuppa Tossa makes this into a riddle tale by stopping before the last paragraph and asking the children how many years man had in all.

Origin Stories

Every culture has its "origin" stories. They work to create a special sense of place. Folks in Luang Prabang, Laos, can look at the mountain Phu Si, standing right in front of the royal palace, and remember the story "Hanuman Gathers Mushrooms." It is interesting to see Hanuman and Sita, well-known from the Indian epics, alighting in Laos too. Climbing Phu Si one day, I could see the palace below and wondered how Sita must have felt when the mountain was suddenly plunked down in front of her!

The Georgians are excessively proud of their heritage. At a *supra* (traditional banquet) I was told the two origin stories in this chapter. "How Georgians Received Their Homeland" is a tale much loved by its people . . . and believed to pronounce the truth about their beautiful country! And "Wine Is Born in Georgia" reaffirms the claim that wine originated in Georgia, a fact for which there is much historical support.

At times, park rangers and other folks leading nature walks tend to get carried away with the need for good origin stories for the spots they are passing. I suspect that the story "The Douglas Fir Cone" is a somewhat modern invention to meet such a need. But it has become so widespread that teachers in the Northwest often ask me for the tale's source. I have elaborated it a bit myself and placed it here. So we see a bit of folk "lore" becoming a folk "tale." Can a folktale be a modern creation? If it gets passed on and changes as it goes, yes, a created tale can enter the folk tradition.

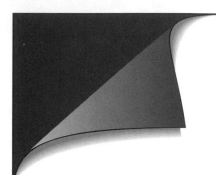

How Georgians Received Their Homeland

A Folktale from The Republic of Georgia

1 minute, 30 seconds

In the beginning God was giving out land to all the peoples.

The Bulgarians came.
"You can live over here."

The Turks came.
"You can live over here."

Now the Georgians were wandering around at that time.
They had come across a really beautiful land.
They found valleys, streams, and good shade under the fig trees.
They saw everything they needed to have a picnic.

So they sat down under the fig trees.
They gathered some fruit, pulled out their bread, opened a jug of wine . . .
and had a *supra,* a feast.
They toasted each other and drank.
They toasted each other and drank.
In fact they drank so much that they all just fell asleep there under the leafy trees.
When they finally work up it was late.

"Uh, oh. Wasn't this the day we were supposed to go see God and get our land?
We'd better hurry!"

When the Georgians came dragging in, God was packing up to leave.
"What! You Georgians! Late again! What on earth were you thinking?
I've already given out all the best land.
And you folks are my favorite people too.
I love people that really know how to live, like you do."

"God, we were having a *supra*. We were toasting *you,* God.
And the time just got away from us."

This tickled God. "Toasting *me,* were you?
Well, I'll tell you what I will do for you.
I had a special spot of land I was keeping for myself to go to when I retire.
But since there isn't any other land left, I will give that garden spot to you
Georgians.
I'll just go live up in the sky myself."

And this is how it happened:
The Georgians got God's own garden!
And they live there to this day.

Told by Nikoloz Baratashivili, of the Tbilisi Youth
Palace, at a *supra* in Tbilisi, Georgia, January 2005. The
supra is a Georgian feast, accompanied by much toasting and drinking of the excellent Georgian wines.

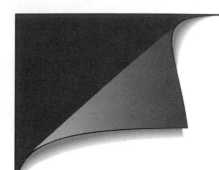

Wine is Born in Georgia

A Folktale from The Republic of Georgia

4 minutes

Once there was and was not . . . has anything *not* been on earth? Well, once there was a time when there *were* grapes on earth . . . but people had no idea how to make wine. Grapevines grew wild in the forests. But only the birds enjoyed their sweet fruit.

Then one day man was passing in the forest and saw those blue grapes. He tasted one. Delicious! So man carefully transplanted a grapevine into his own yard. Now he had grapes every year and invited his friends to come sample them. They were so popular that he planted more vines and soon had a whole vineyard bearing delicious grapes.

But one year the grapes bore so plentifully that he and his friends could not eat them all. What to do? The man decided to make grape juice! He squeezed the juice in clay jars and set it aside for the winter.

Time passed and the grape juice developed some interesting qualities! He invited his friends back to taste the grape juice. Amazing! But should it still be called grape juice?

They all sat down and began to debate the values of this unusual beverage. The animals arrived and wanted to have a say in the matter too.

Seeing all this, the god Bacchus hurried over to act as *tamada* . . . the master of the feast.
He filled a bowl with the rosy liquid and handed the first bowl to Nightingale.

Nightingale took a sip and began to sing.
"Whoever drinks three bowls of this will sing as sweetly as I do!"
Nightingale drank his bowlful and set it down.

Lion filled the bowl and lifted it.
"Whoever drinks five bowls will become as strong and brave as I am!"
He drank his bowlful and set it down.

Next came Locust. Locust filled his bowl.
"Whoever drinks seven bowls will squeak tediously like I do."
Locust drank and set back the bowl.

Dog filled the bowl.
"Whoever drinks nine bowls will growl like I do."
Dog swallowed his bowlful and set it down.

Goose filled the bowl.
"Whoever drinks eleven bowls will be a simpleton . . . just like me!"
Goose drank and put down his bowl.

Then came Pig.
"Whoever drinks TWELVE bowls will roll in the mud, just like me!"

At this point the god Bacchus stood up and filled the bowl for himself.

"You have bestowed on this liquid all of my qualities! My strengths and my frailties! So I will name this liquid. It shall be called 'wine' and shall be my own special drink."

Thus man discovered wine. Man began to cultivate the grapes. He adapted many species for his wine-making. And he learned to make many subtle kinds of the liquid.

But to this day, all wines preserve the qualities given to them by the animals on that long-ago day.

If a man drinks three bowls he will sing as sweetly as a nightingale.

If he drinks five bowls he will find himself as strong and brave as a lion.

But if he drinks seven bowls he will begin to squeak like a locust and tire everyone.

If he drinks nine bowls he will start to growl like a dog.

If he drinks eleven bowls . . . he will be as stupid as the simpleton goose.

And heaven forbid, should he drink twelve bowls . . . you will find him rolling in the mud and grunting . . . just like a pig!

Retold from *Georgian Folk Tales: The Nine Brothers and Other Stories [xuTkunWula da sxva zRaprebi]* (Tbilisi, Georgia: Bakur Sulakauri Publishing, 2004), pp. 45–48. Translated for me by Ketevan Gviniashvili. I also heard great tellings of the tale by Irakli Topuria, Irakli Garibashvili, and others at a *supra* in Tbilisi, winter of 2005. The Georgians insist that Georgia is indeed the birthplace of wine and it seems that every Georgian can tell you a version of this great story of how it all began. In fact, wine vessels dating back to 5000 B.C. have been unearthed in Georgia, as well as seven-thousand-year-old grape stones. A1428 *Acquisition of wine*. A2851 *The four characteristics of wine*. This tale reminds us of B592 *Animals bequeath characteristics to Man*.

The Douglas Fir Cone

A North American Nature-walk Tale

■▪ 1 minute, 40 seconds

Once in the early times there lived a little mouse who was always running
around.
Here . . . there . . . here . . . there . . .
"I've got seeds! "
Here . . . there . . . here . . . there . . .
"I've got more seeds!"

Mouse hid lots of seeds for the winter.
He had a big stash of seeds.
It was time to curl up and wait out the winter.
But Mouse was never satisfied.
"More! More!"
He was still running . . .
Here . . . there . . . here . . . there . . .
"I've got more seeds!
I've got more seeds!"

The days got colder and colder.
But still Mouse did not go down into his hole where he belonged.
Here . . . there . . . here . . . there . . .
"I've got more! I've got MORE!"

On the day when the first big snowstorm struck,
Mouse was far from his hole . . . still gathering seeds.
He had no way to get back to his nice warm hole.
Now Mouse was in big trouble.
"Fir Tree! Fir Tree!
You have to help me!
Open your cones a little.
Let me hide inside.
This storm is too cold for me!"

The Fir Tree was kind.
"Oh course, Little Mouse,
come shelter in my fir cone.
But Little Mouse, promise you won't nibble
on my seeds in there. Okay?"

"Okay, Fir Tree! I promise.
Just let me in!"

So Fir Tree opened her cone,
and Little Mouse crept in.
It was warm and cozy in there.
But after a while Mouse began to feel a bit hungry.
"Fir Tree won't even notice if I eat a seed or two."
And Mouse began to nibble away.

"WHAT are you doing? You PROMISED!"
Fir Tree was angry now.
She clamped her cone shut and trapped Mouse inside.
"Mouse wants to eat my seeds? He can just STAY there."
Oh dear. The greedy mouse was stuck for good inside the fir cone.

Even today, if you look closely at a fir cone
you will see a mouse tail and little mouse feet dangling out of the cone.

Elaborated from various stories told in nature education programs. I found one version on the website of the University
of British Columbia's Botanical Garden and Centre for Plant
Research (www.ubcbotanicalgarden.org.) Additionally, the
sites of the Port Renfew Community (British Columbia),
(www.portrenfrewcommunity.com) and Moab Happenings
event magazine (Utah) (www.moabhappenings.com) provided
variants in which a mouse runs inside a Douglas fir cone to
escape a forest fire. I first heard the story from a lady ranger at
Discovery Park in Seattle circa 1982. Many websites prepared by
naturalists describe the Douglas fir cone as looking like a mouse's
tail and rear end, even though they don't always refer to this story.

The Blacksmith on the Moon

A Lao Folktale from Northeastern Thailand
Retold by Prasong Saihong

 5 minutes

A blacksmith was pounding iron to make knives in front of a hot fire.
Peng . . . peng . . . peng . . .
He was complaining: "I am so unhappy . . .
I don't want to be a blacksmith anymore!"

Then he looked up and saw a large stone standing on the mountain.
And the breeze blew it all the time—
Wee . . . wee . . . wee . . .

"If I could be that stone, I would be so happy!"

Suddenly a *thevada* appeared and said,
        "If he wants that,
            he will have that!"
The *thevada* recited words of incantation.
        "Ohm piang!"

The blacksmith was turned into a stone standing on the mountain.
And the wind blew all around him,
Wee . . . wee . . . wee . . .

"I am so happy now," he thought.
He was so happy until . . .

"Ouch! Ouch! What is this?"

He looked around and saw a stone carver hitting him with a chisel and a hammer.

He complained again:
"Why are you doing this to me?
I am so unhappy . . ."

The blacksmith-stone looked at the stone carver and said,
"If I could be that stone carver, I would be happy."

Suddenly the *thevada* appeared and said,
        "If he wants that,
        he will have that."
The *thevada* recited words of incantation:
        "*Ohm piang!*"

The blacksmith was turned into a stone carver.
And the wind blew all around him,
Wee . . . wee . . . wee . . .

"I am so happy!" he thought.
He was so happy looking for a stone to carve.
But he could not find the right stone to carve.

So he complained again.
"This one is too big! This one is too small!"

The sun was shining so brightly,
and the blacksmith who was the stone carver felt so tired.
He cried out, "I am so unhappy!
I don't want to be a stone carver anymore!"

Then he looked at the sun.
"If I could be the sun, I would be so happy."

Suddenly the *thevada* appeared and said,
        "If he wants that,
        he will have that."
The *thevada* recited words of incantation,
        "*Ohm piang!*"

The blacksmith was turned into the sun.
He was so happy shining early in the morning.
And the wind blew all around him,
Wee . . . wee . . . wee . . .

"I am so happy," he thought.
But when it got later, he began to feel hotter and hotter.
So he shouted, "I am so unhappy!
I don't want to be the sun anymore."

Then he looked across the sky and saw the moon.
"If I could be the moon, I would be so happy."

Suddenly the *thevada* appeared.
      "If he wants that,
        he will have that."
The *thevada* recited words of incantation . . .
        "Ohm piang!"

The blacksmith was turned into the moon!
He was so happy appearing in the sky early that night.
And the wind blew
Wee . . . wee . . . wee . . .

"I am so happy," he thought.
But when it got later and later, he began to feel so cold.
He shouted, "I am so unhappy!
I don't want to be the moon anymore!"

The blacksmith who was now the moon
thought about how hot it was when he was a blacksmith.
And he said, "If I could be the blacksmith I once was,
I would be so happy!"

Suddenly the *thevada* appeared and said,
      "If he wants that,
        he will have that."

The *thevada* recited the words of incantation,
"Ohm piang!"

The blacksmith who was the moon. . . .
turned into the blacksmith he once was.
But now he was not pounding iron on earth.
He was pounding iron on the moon!

And it was so cold there. The blacksmith got so cold
that he had to pound iron in front of a hot fire everyday.

If you look up on the night of the full moon,
You will see the blacksmith pounding on the moon—
Peng . . . peng . . . peng . . .

Well, at least he is not hot anymore!

This story was collected by Prasong Saihong in Mahasarakham
Province, in Northeastern Thailand. Prasong, a member of the
Mahasarakham Storytelling Troupe, shaped the story for sharing
with child audiences. Many more Lao/Isaan folktales may be
found on the website created at Northern Illinois University by
Prasong Saihong and Dr. Wajuppa Tossa (www.seasite.niu.edu/
lao/Lao_Folklore/lao_folklore_course.htm). A *thevada* (teh-
va-DAH) is a divine being. A 751.1 *Man in the moon is person
thrown or sent there as punishment.* Z42 *Stronger and strongest.* L392
Mouse stronger than wall, wind, mountain. A similar chain tale is told
in Japan about a stonecutter. Other versions often feature a mouse
looking for a husband who is strongest. See MacDonald L392 for
versions from Russia, France, Nepal, Korea, India, and Vietnam.
And MacDonald Z42 for similar tales from Japan, India,
Indonesia, China, India, Rumania, Eskimo, Puerto Rico, and
Zanzibar.

Hanuman Gathers Mushrooms

A Folktale from Luang Prabang, Laos
Retold from Wajuppa Tossa

 4 minutes

Long ago the royal palace at Luang Prabang faced a meadow. King Rama and Queen Sita could look out across the fields. There was no mountain in front of the palace blocking its view . . . as there is today.

One morning Queen Sita felt a great hungering for monkey-ear mushrooms. These mushrooms are a special delicacy. But they are hard to find. Queen Sita knew that monkey-ear mushrooms did grow on Udomxai Mountain. But that mountain was far away.

She called her loyal friend, Hanuman the Monkey King. Hanuman had great magical powers, so she knew he could fly easily to Udomxai Mountain to look for mushrooms. But she felt it would offend him if she asked him to bring "monkey-ear" mushrooms. So she just said, "Hanuman, I am hungry for mushrooms today. Would you fly to Udomxai Mountain and bring me some mushrooms?"

"Yes, your majesty." Hanuman flew off.

He looked here and there on Udomxai Mountain and picked a basketful of mushrooms for Queen Sita.

Hanuman flew back and presented the mushrooms to the queen. "Here, your majesty."

Queen Sita looked through the mushrooms. There were no monkey-ear mushrooms in the basket.

"Oh Hanuman. The mushrooms I really want are not here. Could you fly back and pick some more?"

"Yes, your majesty." So Hanuman flew back to Udomxai Mountain and picked another basketful of mushrooms.

"Here, your majesty." Hanuman presented the mushrooms to Queen Sita.

Sita looked through all of the mushrooms. Still there were no monkey-ear mushrooms.

"Dear Hanuman . . . these just aren't the kind of mushroom I want today. Would you go and pick another basket for me?"

Hanuman was getting tired. But he replied patiently, "Yes, your majesty." And he flew back to Udomxai Mountain.

Again the basket did not contain the mushrooms Queen Sita wanted.

Back and forth . . . back and forth . . . flew Hanuman.

At last his patience was wearing thin. "What on earth can she want?" he wondered.

Then Hanuman had an idea.

When he returned he plopped his find right in front of the palace and the queen gasped.

"Why thank, you, Hanuman. I am sure I will have the mushrooms I want now."

Here is a riddle for you: What did Hanuman bring that startled the queen . . . but did provide her with her "monkey-ear" mushrooms?

(Here is the answer: Hanuman simply lifted the entire top off of Udomxai Mountain and brought it back to Luang Prabang. He plopped the mountain top right in front of the palace.)

"Here, your majesty! You can pick any mushrooms you want now!"

So Queen Sita whispered to her servants "Pick me some monkey-ear mushrooms." And soon she had what she wanted.

When Hanuman saw what she had gathered, he was exasperated. "Why didn't you just *ask* for monkey-ear mushrooms?"

"Oh, I didn't want to offend you, my dear Hanuman."

"Well next time . . . please offend me, Queen Sita! It will be a lot less trouble!"

Retold from *Lao Folktales* by Wajuppa Tossa and Kongdeuane Nettavong. (Westport, Connecticut: Libraries Unlimited, 2007). The mountain Hanuman brought is called Phu Si. It stands right in front of the royal palace in Luang Prabang, the old capital of Laos. And they say that the top of Mt. Odomxai is flat— the top having been lifted off by Hanuman long ago when he carried it to Luang Prabang! Sita, Rama, and Hanuman the Monkey King are main characters in the famous Indian epic, The Ramayana. This story is a part of the mythology of Thailand and Laos. The story was related by Ms. Chanphen Singphet of the Children's Cultural Center in Luang Prabang. Dr. Wajuppa Tossa tells this story as a riddle, pausing to let the audience guess what Hanuman brought to finally please the queen. A962.10 *Hills represent loads from culture-hero's shoulders.*

Tiny Tales

Here are some very short tales. "Swimming to Kotzebue" is exactly one minute long. When Lela Kiana Oman told me this little tale I said, "Oh no, Lela! I can't tell that to our children. It has a bad ending!" Lela replied, "You had better tell it! It is an important story to hear. Your children won't be eaten by polar bears, but if they don't learn to pay attention they could be hit by a truck!" So I tell this story all the time.

How would you like to tell a story that is four thousand years old? Well, here is "Toothache"! Tell it to your dentist next time you visit.

"Unity Is Strength" is a short little Georgian tale that shares "Take a Little Walk, Bear" (in the Participation Tales section) from the bee's perspective!

The Basques have many humorous anecdotes about the travels of St. Peter and the Lord. I have given just two of them here. You could find a few Basque tale collections and string together a whole program of such tales.

Many tales point up morals. The Lao tale, "How to Quarrel," does this very concisely.

Swimming to Kotzebue

An Eskimo Tale as told by Lela Kiana Oman

| 1 minute |

Little Mouse was swimming to Kotzebue.
Little Mouse was swimming to Kotzebue to get married.
He was *sooo* happy.
He was *sooo* happy.
Little Mouse was swimming to Kotzebue to get married.

The willow trees on the bank bent over.
"Mouse . . . mouse . . . be careful where you swim.
Don't go near the deep water.
Don't go near the deep water."

Little Mouse was swimming to Kotzebue to get married.
He was *sooo* happy.
He said, "I won't go near the deep water.
I won't go near the deep water.
I'm swimming to Kotzebue to get married!"

Little Mouse was swimming to Kotzebue to get married.
He was *soooo* happy.
He didn't look where he was going.
He swam right into the deep water.
A big pike fish came up and swallowed Little Mouse.
The end.

This story was told to me by Lela Kiana Oman in 1992 at her son's home in Snomohish, Washington. Lela, an Eskimo elder from Nome, Alaska, has published several collections of her people's traditions. Lela told me that her father always told her this story when they were camped out on the tundra in tents during the summertime. There were wolverines and polar bears around. These could eat a little girl. Her father wanted her to always be paying attention . . . even if she was *soooo* happy. So he told her Little Mouse's story every night. You can read more about Lela and her wonderful storytelling traditions in my book *Ten Traditional Tellers* (Bloomington: University of Illinois Press, 2006).

Toothache!

An Assyrian Folktale

 1 minute, 45 seconds

First God created the heavens.
Then the heavens created the earth.
Earth created the rivers.
Rivers created ditches.
Ditches created mud.
And mud created . . . the worm.

But Worm was miserable.
Worm had nothing to eat.
So Worm went to the God of Justice.

Worm cried and cried.
"I am hungry! I am miserable!
I don't want to live in the mud!"

Ea, the God of Wisdom, listened to Worm complaining and complaining.
"Give me something juicy to eat!" cried Worm.
"Give me something delicious to drink!"

"I will please you, Worm," said Ea.
"I will give you ripe figs to eat.
I will give you apricots."

"Who wants ripe figs?" fussed Worm.
"What good are apricots?
I want you to take me out of this mud.
I want to live between the teeth of men.
Let me drink the blood of their jaws.
Let me gnaw on the roots of their teeth.

THAT would be good food!
THAT would be good drink!"

"Well, if that is what you want," said Ea,
"that is what you will get.
You may live right among men's teeth.
You may feast on their jaws.
But I warn you . . .
from now on the mighty hand of Ea will be against you to crush you.
I cannot leave man unprotected."

So to this day the worm lives in the teeth of men.
You might have felt him there.
He gnaws and sucks and makes men miserable.
But always Ea's servant is fighting against that worm . . .
That servant is called . . . the Dentist!

Go see him if you have a toothache.

And also it is said that if the worm is bothering you,
you should take some medicine . . . and recite this story three times.
That should cure you!

Retold from "How Toothache Came into the World"
by Theodor Gaster in *The Oldest Stories in the World*.
(New York: Viking, 1952), pp. 93–96. Gaster cites his
source as *Proceedings of the Society of Biblical Archaeology*,
vol. xxviii, 1906, p. 78, as retold by R. Campbell
Thompson. These stories were first written down
on cuneiform tablets, perhaps as early as 1700 B.C.
Gaster tells us that Ea was considered the god of sci-
ence and worshipped at Eridu (known as Abu Sharein
today). D1502.2.2 *Charm for toothache.*

Unity Is Strength
A Georgian Folktale

▌ 1 minute

Bear was wandering through the forest.
There was an old oak tree.
There was a hollow in the oak tree.
In the hollow the bear could hear something . . .
Bzzzzzz . . .

"I believe I'm hearing bees!" thought Bear.
"I believe they are making honey in there!"
Bear sat down to think about this lucky find.

But just then a bee noticed Bear.
"You had better get away from here, Bear!
We don't want BEARS around our tree!"

"Oh, yes, little Bee. And what are you going to do about it?" scoffed the big bear.

"If you don't leave you will be sorry!" buzzed the bee.

"Sure. Sure . . . ," laughed the big bear.
"A bee really scares ME."

But just then another bee flew out of the tree.
Bzzzzzz . . ."Get out of here, BEAR!"

"A couple of little bees! You won't run ME off."

But then three bees came . . . and four . . . and more . . .
They began to swarm all around the big bear.

From overhead the blackbird called down to Bear.
"You'd better run fast, Bear.
One bee is weak, it is true.
But there is strength in unity.
And there are MANY MANY bees."

Just then the bees began to sting that bear.

"OWWWW!!! You are right, Blackbird!"
And Bear ran as fast as he could away from that tree.

One may be weak . . . but many can conquer.

Retold from *The Lullaby and Other Stories* by Iacob
Gogebashvili (Tbilisi: Ganatleba Publishers, 1991),
p. 36. Gogebashvili was a nineteenth-century
Georgian educator. J624 *Uniting against a common
enemy.* J1020 *Strength in unity.*

St. Peter and the Lord

A Basque Folktale

▌ 40 seconds

One day when Saint Peter and the Lord Jesus were traveling the world, the Lord turned to Saint Peter.

"Tell you what, Saint Peter. I will give you a horse . . . if you can recite the Our Father from beginning to end without letting your thoughts wander."

"Bah! What an easy thing you are asking me to do!" said Saint Peter.

And—*tarrapatan!*—Saint Peter started praying. "Our father. Which art in heaven. Hallowed by thy name . . . By the way, Lord . . . will the horse have a saddle too?"

"Too bad!" laughed the Lord. "Now you will get neither saddle nor horse. You couldn't keep your mind fixed on the prayer for even three seconds!"

The Basques tell many stories about Saint Peter and the Lord on their wanderings through Basque country. This one is from *A Book of the Basques* by Rodney Gallup (Reno: University of Nevada Press, 1970), p. 173. Gallup's source was "Don Joni Petriren Zaldia" in *Gure Herria* (1923). Type 774 *Jests about Christ and Peter. Peter made ridiculous.* K1811 *Gods (saints) in disguise visit mortals.*

The Slovenly Wife

A Basque Folktale

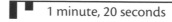

1 minute, 20 seconds

At the time when the Lord Jesus and Saint Peter were wandering through the Basque lands they were once very hot and thirsty. At a spring they met a woman in dirty, torn clothing. "Could you pour a glass of water for thirsty travelers?" asked the Lord.

The woman poured water into two filthy old glasses and handed them over. Jesus drank of the water and handed the glass back to the woman. "May God give you a good husband," he said. And the two went on their way.

Later, being thirsty again, they stopped at another spring. Here a tidily dressed woman in well-cared-for clothing served them. The water was in a clean glass.

When the Lord handed back the glass he said, "May God give you a slovenly husband."

They had gone on only a few steps when Saint Peter spoke crossly to Jesus. "What on earth were you thinking back there? You promised a good husband to that *dirty* woman and a slovenly husband to the second, who was so *clean!*"

"Well," replied Jesus, "The first woman will have trouble keeping up with things even with a good husband to help her. The second woman will be quite capable of keeping even a slovenly husband in order. Thus we will end with two happy families."

Translated from "Emazteki Zirtzila eta Emazteki Garbia" in *Gure Herria* (1922) and reprinted in *A Book of the Basques* by Rodney Gallup (Reno: University of Nevada Press, 1970), p. 174. Type 774 *Jests about Christ and Peter. Peter made ridiculous.* K1811 *Gods (saints) in disguise visit mortals.* Compare this story with "The Queen and the Peasant Wife" on page 145.

How to Quarrel
A Folktale from Laos

 2 minutes

Once the king heard of a couple who would always quarrel.
"Let us see if this quarreling can be stopped," said the king.
So he sent men with one hundred pieces of silver to their house.
"If the two of you can pass one day without quarreling, this silver is yours."

"Then we must find a way not to quarrel!" exclaimed the husband.
"Wife, you must hold your tongue with your hand all day today.
Otherwise there is no way you will get through the day without arguing
with me."

"Well, even if I do not say one word . . ." responded his wife,
"there will still be quarreling in this house.
All the neighbors *know* that you are the one who quarrels all the time."

And with that the two began to argue.
The king's men laughed and carried away the silver.
This couple would never learn to stop arguing.

The king thought to test another couple the same way.
He had heard that this couple never ever argued.
So the king sent his men to their house with a different command.
"If the two of you will become angry with each other today,
we will give you this pile of silver."

The husband wanted the silver.
So he thought of a way to annoy his wife.
He wove a basket for her spinning cotton that had so many holes in it that
the cotton could just blow out.

But when he gave the basket to the wife, she just smiled gently.
"Well, look at this basket. The sun can come right in and warm the cotton. How nice."

So the husband wove her a basket with a top so narrow that her hand would be scratched in getting the cotton out.
"This will surely make her mad, " he thought.
"She will say cross things to me now."

But his wife just smiled sweetly.
"Well, look at this basket. The wind will never blow the cotton out of this, no matter how hard it blows. Thank you, husband."

The king's men had been hiding all day, watching this couple.
They saw now that this couple just did not know how to quarrel.
So they returned to the king and told the story.

"Then they shall have the silver pieces," said the king,
"for such a peace-loving couple is rare indeed."

Retold from *Laos Folk-Lore of Farther India* by
Katherine Neville Fleeson (New York: Fleming H.
Revell, 1899), pp. 105–107. A1375.1 *Why some married
people quarrel.* T256 *The quarrelsome wife or husband.*
Q306 *Quarrelsomeness punished.*

Riddle Tales

I included a section of riddle tales in my previous book, *Three-Minute Tales*. But I keep finding more fun examples to share.

"The Little Red House" is a story known to most preschool teachers. There are probably as many variants as there are teachers! I combined several to make my own here. It can be told as a riddle for the children to guess, or just told as a story without the interactive question-and-answer. You do need a ripe red apple and a knife to make the story work!

Dr. Wajuppa Tossa had fun telling "The Serving Giant" in schools in the Seattle area last year. She managed to get some amazing answers to her riddle. In fact the answers she elicited were much more interesting than the riddle answer in the story itself!

Math riddles are a challenge. Folklorist Inta Carpenter heard "How Many Geese?" from her Latvian grandfather. See if you can solve it without looking at the answer.

If you like riddle tales, you should enjoy the books by George Shannon: *Stories to Solve* (New York: HarperCollins, 1985); *More Stories to Solve* (New York: Greenwillow, 1990); *Still More Stories to Solve* (New York: Greenwillow, 1994); *True Lies* (New York: Greenwillow, 1997); and *Still More True Lies* (New York: Greenwillow, 2001). I use these to teach storytelling to beginners. I pass out one riddle tale to each student and give them five minutes to read and think about it. Then I tell them to go face one of the walls in the classroom and start telling their story out loud. After five minutes I exhort them to project their voices and add gestures. After another five minutes we come back together and share our stories.

Since they don't have to tell the end, the rest of the class guesses at the answer, and the tale telling is easy—a surefire way to telling success!

The Little Red House

An American Folk Story

 4 minutes, plus guessing time

One autumn day a little boy sat watching the leaves drift in the wind.
He wanted something to do.
"I have an idea," said his mother.
"Here is a riddle:

> A little red house.
> No doors.
> No windows.
> A star inside.

You will find it somewhere on our farm.
But I won't tell you where to look.
And if you find the answer . . . I will make you a pie!"

The boy started off to look for this "little red house."
He had never seen anything like that on the farm.
What could the riddle mean?

A plump hen crossed his path.
"Hen! I have a riddle.
Have you ever seen . . .

> A little red house.
> No doors.
> No windows.
> A star inside."

"*Cluck! Cluck!* What nonsense!"
"There's no such thing!"
And the hen strutted off.

Here came Cat.
"Cat, can you help solve my riddle?

A little red house.
No doors.
No windows.
A star inside."

Cat thought about this.
"*Meow! Meow!* That's nonsense!
There is no such thing!"
And the cat strolled away with her tail in the air.

"Well, someone must be able to help."
The boy started across the field.
"Sheep! Can you solve my riddle?
    A little red house.
    No doors.
    No windows.
    A star inside."

"*Baaa! Baaa!*" bleated the sheep.
"That is nonsense!
There is no such thing!"

Surely someone must know, thought the boy.
"Cow! Come help me solve my riddle.
    A little red house.
    No doors.
    No windows.
    A star inside.
What could it be?"

"*Mooo! Mooo!* How should I know?
It sounds like nonsense.
There is no such thing."

Boy climbed the hill to ask Horse.
Horse was standing under the apple tree, munching on the ripe, red apples.

"Horse! Help me solve my riddle.

A little red house.
No doors.
No windows.
A star inside."

Horse thought about this.
"These apples are little.
These apples are red.
And they make a nice house for a worm.
But I never noticed a star inside."

Little Boy picked up an apple from the ground.
It was red.
It certainly didn't have any doors or windows.
And it was true . . . worms lived in some of the apples.
But a star inside?

Little Boy carried the apple home to his mother.
"This can't be the answer to the riddle,
but Horse said . . ."

His mother laughed and picked up the bright red apple.
"Well, let's see if we can find a star inside," she said.
She cut the apple right in half.
And . . . there . . . was the star!

"And now . . ." said his mother,
"I will make you your pie. An apple pie!"

When a patron at the Bothell Library asked for a copy of the "apple story" one fall, I put out a query over our system e-mail. At once I received seven different versions of this story! Thanks to all the King County Library System children's librarians who shared their versions of this tale. The story can be expanded or contracted by adding in more animals to meet on the way. Some versions replace the animals with humans: boy, girl, farmer, Granny, etc. Several have the wind blow the apple down to the boy. To reveal the star, you must cut the apple crosswise. Lie it on its side and slice right through the middle, the opposite of the usual way of slicing an apple from stem to bottom. The seeds form a star around the apple's core. To make this into a riddling story, you can let the children try to guess the answer before the boy approaches the horse. Then go ahead and tell the ending.

The Serving Giant
A Lao Tale retold from Wajuppa Tossa

 4 minutes, plus guessing time

A poor farmer was once digging in his field when . . . *Bonk!*
His hoe struck something hard.
"What could it be?" he thought.

He dug . . . and soon unearthed a large jar.
"Oh, this might be like in the old stories!
Maybe it is full of gold!"

The farmer was so excited.
He quickly pulled off the lid of the jar.
Whoosh! A cloud of smoke rushed out of the jar!

The farmer shrank back in fright.
Then . . . the cloud of smoke began to form itself . . . into the shape of an enormous GIANT!
The farmer dropped to his knees in terror.

But the giant simply bowed and put his hands together respectfully in a polite *wai:*
"Master, I have come to serve you.
I will do any task you ask."

The farmer sat up. This sounded good!
"But I must warn you," continued the giant,
"if you do not keep me busy . . . I will have to eat you."
The man was terrified all over again.
"No problem," said the giant.
"As long as I have something to do, I can control my urge to gobble you up."

80

The farmer thought . . ."I can use help on my farm.
I am sure I can keep this creature busy."
So he ordered: "Remove all the rocks from this field. And hoe the entire garden."

"Yes, Master."

The giant chanted . . ."*Ohm piang!*"
In an instant, the rocks were removed and the garden was hoed.
"Finished, Master. Next task?"

The farmer hadn't thought the giant could do this task so quickly.
This time, he had better think of something that would take longer.

"Uhhh . . . Giant, build me a house. It must be built of wood from the distant forest . . . The wood must be selected with care . . . The walls must be . . ." The farmer gave many directions.

"Yes, Master."

"This should take him quite a while," thought the farmer.

But . . . "*Ohm piang!*"
A new house stood before the farmer.
"Finished, Master. Next task?"

All day long the farmer thought up task after task for the giant.
But no matter how complicated the work, the giant completed it in a flash.

"*Ohm piang!*"
"Finished, Master. Next task?"

The farmer was desperate.
As long as he was awake, he could keep thinking up tasks for the giant.
But as soon as he fell asleep, the giant would run out of chores and . . .
eat him!

Suddenly the farmer had an inspiration!
He issued an order that the giant could never complete!
Then he lay down and fell asleep with relief.

Here is the riddle:
>   What was the order that the farmer gave to the giant?
>   What task could he never complete?

(Audience members come up with fascinating answers to this riddle . . . Their answers are actually more interesting than the story's answer! Here are some that have been given: a monk in Vientianne suggested the giant should be told to study, because studying is endless. Dr. Wajuppa's university students, who were being forced to read many English-language children's books, suggested that the giant be told to "Read all the children's books in the world!" A student at Westhill Elementary in Bothell, Washington, suggested that the giant be ordered to stand guard as a scarecrow! My storytelling friend Meg Lippert suggested asking the giant to tell an endless story! See what your audiences can come up with. The fun of this tale is in their many answers.)

The answer that comes with the story?
The farmer told the giant to set a pole forty meters tall in front of his house and to climb to the top, then come back down, then climb up again . . . and not stop until the farmer gave the order to quit. The giant is still climbing up and down the pole to this day.

Told by Pha Sunantha Theerapanyophikkhu, Vientiane, Laos. A retelling by Dr. Wajuppa Tossa appears in *Lao Tales* by Wajuppa Tossa and Kongdeuane Nettavong (Westport, Connecticut: Libraries Unlimited, 2007). The giant in the story is a *yak*. If you have visited Bangkok, envision the glittering royal giants standing guard at the temples there. E454 *Ghost laid by giving it a never-ending or impossible task.* N813 *Helpful genie (spirit).* K551 *Respite from death until particular act is performed.* D1421.1 *Magic object summons genie.* G307 *Jinn.* H1010 *Impossible tasks.*

How Many Geese?
A Latvian Riddle Tale

▌ 45 seconds, plus guessing time

There is a big old frog pond out behind my grandpa's house. One day I was sitting on the bank out there, and a whole flock of geese flew up and landed in the pond. They were swimming around and squawking when one last goose came flapping up.

"Hey!" called that last goose. "Looks like a HUNDRED geese down in that pond!"

The geese all looked up at that goose circling above.
The lead goose stretched out his long neck and called,

"No way are we one hundred geese!
But if you doubled our number . . .
Then added half our number to that . . .
Then added one fourth our number to that . . .
And then you come join us . . .
we *would* be one hundred geese.
Now . . . just how many geese are we?"

(The answer is 36. The algebraic equation would be
$2X + \frac{1}{2}X + \frac{1}{4}X + 1 = 100$)

From *Folklore in the Classroom* by Betty J. Belanus (Bloomington, Indiana: Folklore in the Classroom Project, n.d.). The story was contributed by Folklorist Inta Carpenter, who heard the riddle from her Latvian grandfather, Jānis Pļavenieks. He said stories like this gave him something to do at night "when I sleep without sleeping." He would lie awake and figure out the solution to puzzle stories that he hadn't thought about for years. Carpenter's master's thesis discusses his storytelling: *A Latvian Storyteller: The Repertoire of Jānis Pļavenieks* (Bloomington: Indiana University, 1975).

The Stolen Boat
A Riddle Tale from Thailand

■ 45 seconds, plus guessing time

Once two men claimed that the same boat was theirs. The case was taken to the judge. After hearing the case, the judge declared that one of these men was lying.

"We cannot have liars in our village," said the judge.
"I will find out which of you is telling the truth."

The judge ordered the boat to be cut in half. Then he sent half of the boat home with each man. The judge accompanied them to observe what happened at each home.

When one man arrived home, his son cried out, "Daddy, why do you have only half a boat?"

When the other man arrived home, his son also cried out. But what he said convinced the judge that this man was innocent.

What did the son say?

(Answer: "Daddy, what happened to the other half of our boat?")

Told by Nang Jian Pumtip, age 66, from
Mahasarakham Province, Thailand. Translated
by Uraiwan Prabipu. Collected by Uraiwan
Prabipu, 1996.

Romances

The beautiful ñandutí lace of Paraguay comes with a haunting tale, "The Origin of Ñandutí Lace," which explains its origin in the spider's web. There are many versions of this legend, but all are sad.

"The Flute Player of the Rice Fields" relates a theme familiar in the folk literature of many Asian countries: that of a human who falls in love with a heavenly being. In this case the story also explains the origins of rice.

I love the Sumatran tale of Princess Pinang Masak. This is a clever and bold young woman who finds a way to escape the clutches of a lecherous ruler. So I suppose rather than being a tale of romance . . . this is a tale of the *escape* from romance!

The Origin of Ñandutí Lace

A Legend from Paraguay

 2 minutes, 30 seconds

Once, long ago, there lived a beautiful Guaraní girl.
She was to be wed to the chief's son,
and the two were very much in love.

But the chief's son wanted to give her a wonderful present for the wedding.
So he took his bow and arrows and went into the forest in search of a
jaguar.
He would bring his love the skin of a jaguar!

It did not worry him that the jaguar is a fierce and magical creature.
He was determined to get a jaguar skin for his bride.
So he set off for the forest.

He made his way cautiously through the forest,
but night came on him and still he had not encountered a jaguar.

Never mind.
The chief's son was self-reliant.
Taking some liana vines dangling from a tall tree,
he tied them together and created for himself a hammock.
Then he climbed into this hammock, hanging from a huge forest tree.
Here he assumed he would be safe to sleep.
But even a chief's son can make a bad decision.

Back in the village, the girl waited and waited for her loved one to return.
He did not.
Days passed.

Men from the village searched the forest for him.
But they found nothing.

It was many years later . . .
a hunter from the tribe stumbled onto a huge tree deep in the forest.
Hanging from the tree were two skeletons . . .
that of a man . . .
and that of a jaguar.
There, at the foot of the tree were the bow and arrows of the young man.

But the young man's skeleton was wrapped tightly in a beautifully woven
cloth.

The spiders of the forest had come together to create a funeral shroud for
this poor young man . . .
such a shroud as his fiancée would have made for him, had she been there.

The woman, widowed before she was even married,
had never lost her sadness.
On hearing of her lover's shroud,
she felt jealous of the spider weavers.
She could not stand the thought that others had woven the death shroud
for her love.

So she went into the forest,
and there, by the side of her lover's bones,
she watched.

Every time the wind and rain destroyed a part of the cloth,
the spiders would set to work and weave that piece again,
even more beautifully than before.

The woman sat day and night, watching closely as the tiny spiders wove.
Through her patience and steadfastness she learned the art of the spiders.
She copied each thing they did.
And at last . . . she herself had woven a shroud for her love—
a shroud just as beautiful as that of the spiders.

It was only then that she allowed his body to be returned to the village and
buried . . .
in the shroud she had woven.

From the love of this woman
and the patience and steadfastness of her work,
came the art of ñandutí lace.
This art is practiced by Guaraní women until this day in Paraguay.

Retold from *Ñandutí* by Gustavo González
(Asunción, Paraguay: Biblioteca del Centro de
Estudios Antropologicos del Ateneo Paraguayo, 1967),
p. 37. Retold there from "La Leyenda del Ñandutí" by
Nicolas Aimot in *El Orden* III-12–1927, Asunción.
The story was heard from an old Guaraní woman liv-
ing in the vicinity of Pirivevyi. A1465 *Origin of decora-
tive art.* MacDonald A1465.2.1★ *Origin of lace making.
Girl finds husband killed in battle has been shrouded in spider web. She weaves a delicate lace shroud imitating the spider's web.* MacDonald A1465.2.1.1★ *Origin of ñandutí
lace. Boy saves spider from drowning. Later he competes for
hand of girl. Most exquisite gift to win her. The spider spins
him a lace mantilla.* Both of the stories cited are
Paraguayan. The source from which I took this tale
included eight versions. In all of these the lover is
covered with a spider-spun shroud. In all except the
one I chose for retelling, he is killed by a rival for the
girl's hand. For a Hawaiian version of weaving from
spider web see MacDonald A1453.2.1★ *Origin of
weaving. Man copies spider and devises art of weaving.* For
a West African (Fan) tale see MacDonald A1457.3.1★
*Origin of the net for fishing. Man copies spider making
webs and makes nets to catch animals.*

The Flute Player
of the Rice Fields

A Folktale from Bali, Indonesia

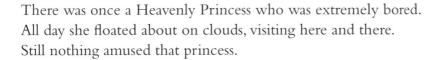 2 minutes, 45 seconds

There was once a Heavenly Princess who was extremely bored.
All day she floated about on clouds, visiting here and there.
Still nothing amused that princess.

One evening as she was drifting about,
she heard a most wondrous melody rising from a small Javanese valley.
Drifting down, the princess saw that the music was coming from the flute
of a rice farmer.

She came closer . . . There she saw the most beautiful man she had ever seen!
"Oh! What is this I feel? Oh!"
The Heavenly Princess fell in love with the flute-playing rice farmer!

Settling down onto the earth,
she picked an armful of red flowers and walked toward the rice farmer.
"Your music is so beautiful.
Let me offer you these flowers."

The young man took one look at this Heavenly Princess carrying flowers,
and he fell in love!

All day the two sat and stared into each other's eyes.
"Ahhhhhh."

That night the Heavenly Princess went to her father.
"Father, I have found the one I will marry."

"Excellent," said her father. "It is time you were getting married.
Call all of the nobles to hear this wonderful announcement."

When everyone was gathered, her father spoke to her:
"Now, tell us the name of the god you choose to marry."

"It is no god, father. It is a beautiful rice farmer I have seen on earth."

"Everyone out!" bellowed her father.
And when the court was cleared, he turned to his daughter.
"You will not marry a human rice farmer.
Not now and not ever.
Go to your room!
And forget about this rice farmer!"

The Heavenly Princess went to her room.
But she did not forget about her rice farmer.

The very next day she floated to where he was playing his flute.
"Aaaahhhh. Such beautiful music.
Such a beautiful young man."

She drifted down beside him.
And once again the two sat staring into each other's eyes.
"Ahhhhhhh."

Soon her father came storming down out of the heavens.
"Back to the palace! I order you!"

"I will never return," said the Heavenly Princess.
"I love this rice farmer.
I will stay here by his side forever."

"Very well," said her father.
"You will stay by his side forever.
But you will not marry a human."

And he turned her into a tall, green rice plant.
The plant was slender and beautiful, just as she had been.
It swayed gracefully in the breeze.

The lovesick rice farmer would not leave the side of that rice plant.
All day and all night, he sat beside her and played loving strains on his flute.

When her father saw that the two could not be separated,
he came down to earth once more.
"I cannot allow you to marry.
But I *will* allow you to remain together.
And so . . . he turned the young man also into a plant of rice.

In the wind, the two turned this way and that,
brushing their leaves together with a sound like sighing.
"Aaahhhhhh."

On the island of Bali,
when the rice is tall and ready for harvest,
you can hear the breeze through the tops of the grain.
If you listen carefully you might hear a sound like music . . .
a sound almost like that of a flute.

A delightful picture book version of this story is *The Princess of the Rice Fields* by Hisako Kimishima, illustrated by Sumiko Mizushi (New York: Walker/ Weatherhill, 1970). This story refers to dry rice, not to wet rice. Dewi Sri is goddess of the wet rice. For more stories of Indonesian rice goddesses see *Indonesian Folktales* by Murti Bunanta (Westport, Connecticut: Libraries Unlimited, 2003). A433.1.1 *God of rice-fields.* D214.1 *Transformation: man to rice grain.* MacDonald A2695.6 *Origin of rice* cites yet two more Indonesian origin-of-rice tales.

Princess Pinang Masak

A Folktale from Indonesia
Retold from Murti Bunanta

 5 minutes

The Princess Pinang Masak was the most beautiful girl in her village.
Word of her beauty soon spread.
Everyone in the entire region knew of her beauty.
Her fame reached far beyond the bounds of her father's small realm.
Soon the Sultan of Sumatera heard of her beauty.

Now the Sultan of Sumatera held sway over the entire island.
He could have anything and anyone he wanted.
And when he heard of a beautiful young girl . . . he wanted *her.*

So when word came to his palace of the faraway Princess Pinang Masak,
he at once sent soldiers to capture her and bring her to his palace.
The sultan already had a harem with more than a hundred beautiful girls
held captive.
But he was eager to add another.

Fortunately, word reached Princess Pinang Masak that the king was sending
soldiers.
She thought long about how she could escape them . . . and she came up
with a plan.

The princess boiled the dark, purple blooms of the banana tree in a huge
vat of water.
Then she began to streak that dark dye onto her skin.
She rubbed it all over her arms.
She rubbed it all over her face, her neck, her shoulders.
She rubbed it all over her legs and feet.

Then she mussed up her hair . . . stuck sticks, straw, and bugs in it.
And she put on the oldest, most ragged clothes she could find.

When the soldiers came to take her . . . they stopped in their tracks.
"This is the beautiful Princess Pinang Masak?"

"There must be some mistake."
This girl is *horrible* to look at!"

But they took her with them all the way back to the sultan's palace.
There they presented her to the sultan.

"What is this hideous object?" exclaimed the sultan.
"This is the Princess Pinang Masak?
Take her out of my sight!
I cannot stand such ugliness!"

So the Princess Pinang Masak was sent back to her own village.
She had outsmarted the sultan.

But of course, in time her skin returned to normal.
She combed her hair and put on beautiful clothing again.
And word of her beauty once more began to travel throughout the island
of Sumatera.

"Have you heard of the Princess Pinang Masak?
She is the most beautiful girl this country has ever seen!"

Soon the sultan heard of this.
"Something is not right here.
The girl I saw was hideous.
Yet I keep hearing of her beauty."

The sultan sent a spy to the home of Princess Pinang Masak.
The man came there incognito and just hung around to see what he could
discover.

One day he saw a most beautiful young lady out walking with her four
girlfriends.

"Who is that girl?" he asked.
"She is amazingly beautiful."

"Oh that is our Princess Pinang Masak."

"That is the Princess Pinang Masak?"
The spy hurried back to inform the sultan.

"Then I have been tricked!" cried the sultan.
He sent a whole contingent of soldiers to arrest the princess at once.

When she heard that soldiers were coming again,
the princess knew she could not fool the sultan a second time.

She and her four girlfriends went down to the water and found a boat.
Two strong young men went with them.
In the dead of night the seven friends escaped from their village.
They sailed down and down . . .
        the whole length of Sumatera . . .
            looking for a place to land.
At last they found a cove that looked promising.
There was fresh water there.
The hills were covered with fruit trees.
And the sea was full of life.
They could live here and create their own village.

The princess changed her name to Princess Senura.
And they called their new village Senura Village.

The sultan never discovered her.

For the rest of their lives the seven lived in this spot.
They married with people from nearby villages,
and their own small village thrived.

When Princess Senura was old and about to die,
she called all the villagers to her.

"I am going to ask a boon of the gods," she told them.
"I am going to ask that no girl in this village should ever be born as beautiful as I was.
That sort of beauty can be a great curse for the girl and her family."

And her wish came true.
To this day the girls of Senura Village are not at all beautiful.

Some say this is a curse.
But some say it is a blessing.

For it means that whenever a girl of Senura Village is asked to marry,
she knows that the young man has not chosen her because he was blinded by her beauty.
He has chosen her because he loves her true self.

It is said that the graves of the Princess Senura, her four girlfriends, and the two young men who accompanied them can still be seen in Senura Village. This story is retold from *Indonesian Folktales* by Murti Bunanta (Westport, Connecticut: Libraries Unlimited, 2003), pp. 48–49. The tale is from Senura village in South Sumatera Province. This is motif K1821.7.1 *Beautiful woman blackens face as disguise.* This is found in the folklore of India. Also D1871 *Girl magically made hideous.*

Strange
and Stranger

Weird tales always have an allure. "The Reader and His Strange Visitors" appeals to me as a librarian. After all, it features a guy with a book who cannot be bothered by ghosts!

"The Girl Who Crunched Bones" is a serious and sad tale, but it shows how a community can bring a lost soul back from the edge. Though it is from a folktale collection, it feels as if it might be a remembered account of an actual event.

When canning factories first appeared in Thailand they seemed just too weird. So here is a tall tale that makes them even weirder! Supaporn Vathanaprida heard this story during the 1950s in her hometown of Lampang. Pineapple and sugar-cane factories, an electrical plant, and a pottery factory had just appeared on the scene there.

"The Rabbit Flood" is a most unusual flood story, featuring a rabbit who can restore felled forests . . . and naughty angels who are punished for eating meat. A very pro-vegetarian tale!

Such amazing tales are found among the peoples of the Amazon. Untainted by the body of world folk literature, some truly unique stories have arisen in this area. "The Magic Canoe" is such a tale. With its ecological message it could have found a place in my *Earth Care* book (Little Rock: August House, 2005) had I seen it in time.

From the Brazilian teller Livia de Almeida comes the truly frightening tale of "The Creature of the Night." I have heard Livia tell this, and she creates quite a feeling of horror by the tale's end. Don't tell it at night. And don't let anyone knock on the door just as you finish.

The Reader and
His Strange Visitors
A Folktale from Korea

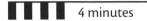 4 minutes

There was once a retired captain who lived all alone.
He had always been an intrepid soul . . .
He had been afraid of nothing when he was out at sea,
and he was afraid of nothing now that he was on land.

This captain loved to read.
Every night he would sit by his fireplace
with a good book in his hands.

On the night our story takes place,
the captain was sitting before his fire, reading as usual.
Outside a storm was brewing . . . whipping the trees into a fury.

Suddenly there was a *thump* at the door.
Something large and black clumped right through the closed door.
The captain stared.
This "thing" looked like a tree stump all wrapped in black mourning cloth.

The "thing" hopped slowly across the floor and sat itself down between the
captain and the fireplace.

"What a strange visitor," said the captain.
And he went on reading.

After a bit there was another *thump* at the door.
And a second "thing" came in.
Slowly it hopped itself across the floor and sat down beside the first.

The captain glanced at it.
"Another visitor, I see."
And he went on reading.

But soon . . . another *thump* at the door.
And a third "thing" came in.
It hopped across the floor and sat itself down beside the other two.

"These visitors are strange enough," muttered the captain.
But he kept on reading his book.

Then the strange visitors began to move.
Closer and closer to the captain they moved . . .
Until they were pressing up against his feet.

The captain pushed his chair back a bit and went on reading.

Closer came the visitors.

The captain pushed his chair back and kept on reading.

Closer still . . .
Every time the captain moved his chair . . .
the "things" came close again.

At last his chair was backed up against the wall.
There was no where else to move.
And there were these horrid "things"
pushed up against his legs.

The captain slapped shut his book.
"*What* do you want?"

"Hungry . . ." said the first visitor.
"Hungry . . ." howled the second visitor.
"Hungry . . ." moaned the third visitor.

"Well, look in the cupboard," said the captain.
"There is food there."

The captain got up to go open the cupboard,
but the things surrounded him.

"Hungry for YOU!"

"Hungry for YOU!"

"Hungry for YOU!"

"Oh you want to eat *me,* do you?"

The captain brought his book up high and *whacked* it down onto the first
thing.
But his book went right through it.

"Out of my house!"

He *whacked* the second thing.
His book went right through it.

He *whacked* the third thing harder with his book.
But the book went through that one too.

And before the captain could think what to try next . . .
something snatched his feet out from under him . . .
and he hit the floor with such a *whack* that it knocked him out.

When the captain came to . . .
he found himself stretched out on the floor.

The wind had died down.
The rain had stopped.
The three "things" had vanished.

The captain slowly picked himself up.
"Was it all a dream?"

He looked around the room.
"Well, if it was a dream . . .
why is my chair pushed way over here by the back wall?"

The captain pulled his chair back up to the fire.
He sat down and picked up his book.
"May the good spirits protect us from any more such visitors!" he
muttered.
And the captain began to read.

Inspired by "Strange Visitors" in *A Book of Spooks and
Spectres* by Ruth Manning-Sanders (New York:
Dutton, 1979), pp. 115–117. Related to H1411 *Fear
test: staying in haunted house.* E440 *Walking ghost "laid."*
This is an example of the way stories distort themselves as they travel. I had photocopied this tale out
from a book by Manning-Sanders, but the top half of
the first page was blurred. Her use of a chair and a
fireplace, as well as the language of her telling, seemed
so British that I assumed the tale was too. Preparing
these notes, I went back to her book. It turns out that
she cites the tale as Korean! She doesn't cite her
source, so I couldn't track this further.

The Girl Who Crunched Bones

A Folktale from Zambia

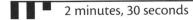 2 minutes, 30 seconds

There was this girl.
Every day she went into the bush.
Every evening she returned.
Her mother called her.
"Here, come and eat.
Here is good food for you."

The girl replied, "No.
I am not hungry."

Each day it was this way.
The mother worried.
"How can my daughter refuse to eat?
How can she live like this?"

The mother went to a person for aid.
"Here is a magic herb.
Put this in your mouth.
When you call,
your daughter must answer.
This way you can discover her.
In the day she does something.
You must find out."

The next day the girl left her home.
The mother waited.
Then she put the herb in her mouth.
She walked into the bush and began to call.

"Kambilocho! Kambilocho! Tuuu!
The daughter answered from over there.
"Kukutu . . . kukutu . . . kukutu . . .
I am crunching bones.
Kukutu . . . kukutu . . . kukutu . . .
Crunching people's' bones."

The mother ran home in terror.
They said, "What happened? What happened?"
"My daughter, she made sounds like crunching bones!
Her voice came from that place . . . that place where graves are made."
They said, "We will go with you."
All walked to that place.
They said, "Keep calling.
You are her mother.
She will know your voice."

The mother called her daughter
"Kambilocho! Kambilocho! Tuuuu!"

From a distance she heard the response.
"Kukutu . . . kukutu . . . kukutu . . . pm!
I am crunching bones.
Kukutu . . . kukutu . . . kukutu . . . pm!
Crunching people's bones."

"That's her," they said.
"Call her. You are her mother."

"Kambilocho! Kambilocho! Tuuu!"

"Kukutu . . . kukutu . . . kukutu . . . pm!
I am crunching bones.
Kukutu . . . kukutu . . . kukutu . . . pm!
Crunching people's bones."

Now they were very close, those people.
That girl was busy crunching.
They crept all around her.
Strong women.
They grabbed her.
Her mother touched her hand,
They carried that girl home.

Back home, they surrounded her.
All good things they brought for her.
After a while she began to take porridge.
A little.
Then more.

They kept her in the village.
They surrounded her and comforted her
until she was able to eat porridge like all other people.
This mother saved her child
with the help of her village.

Retold from "The Child Who Puzzled Her Mother"
by W.F.D. Sakala, a Nyanja folktale in *Folktales from
Zambia* by Dorothea Lehman (Berlin: Verlag von
Dietrich Reimer, 1983). Published also in *The Healing
Heart: Communities* edited by Allison M. Cox and
David H. Albert (Gabriola Island, British Columbia:
New Society Publishers, 2003). P232 *Mother and
daughter.* G30 *Person becomes cannibal.* G33.1 *Cannibal
disenchanted by overcoming it. Becomes maiden.* Type 406
The Cannibal. A couple have a child who is a cannibal.

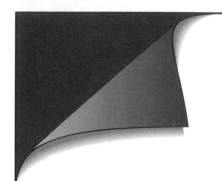

The Marvelous Canning Factory

A Folktale from Northern Thailand
Retold from Supaporn Vathanaprida

 2 minutes, 45 seconds

Have you ever heard of the world's most advanced canning factory?
It was built recently near here.
Such a canning factory has never been seen before.
Fresh food is dumped into one end of the machine.
That machine will wash, clean, chop, separate, and can the food . . .
all by itself!

People have been coming from far and wide to see this marvelous canning factory.
They just shake their heads in bewilderment when they see it in action.
I haven't seen the machine yet, myself, but each person who goes to see it comes back with the most fabulous canning-factory story heard yet.

One person told me,
"These machines were so advanced.
The workers fed raw bananas into them, still on the stalk.
In just minutes, the bananas came out the other end completely processed.
There were dried bananas, deep-fried bananas,
barbecued bananas, and sugar-coated bananas.
All from that one bunch of raw bananas.
I tried some of them.
They were delicious!"

The next visitor saw even more wonders.
"What you saw was fascinating, but not as wonderful as the things I saw.
When I toured the factory, they were feeding the machines live,
pregnant pigs.
Within minutes, these pigs came out as five-starred pork soup and barbecued pork.

106

The unborn piglets came out as crispy, barbecued pork-on-stick with garlic.
The pork fat was all separated and put into containers,
and the skin and bones were turned into fertilizer, packaged in equally
weighted sacks."

But a third visitor had an even more fabulous story to tell.
"The day that I toured the factory,
we arrived as it was getting dark late in the afternoon.
They were herding cows into the machines to make canned meat for
the army.
The manager was busy with guests and could not attend to the machines.

"After the manager finished with his guests,
he came to the machines and tasted the canned meat.
It was too bland.
Someone had forgotten to push the buttons for salt and fish sauce.
The manager stopped the work right away.
'Put all of this canned food back into the machines,' he said.
'We must add in the salt and fish sauce.'
Then he looked at his watch.
'It is too late to process all of this today.
We will wait until tomorrow to can it again.'

"So the workers put all of the canned meat back into the machine.
They pushed the reverse button on the machine,
and the machine began to run again.
Only this time, it worked backwards.
Into the back end of the machine went the canned meat.
Out the front end of the machine backed the whole cows.
All of those cows walked back out to their pasture,
where they continued to graze until the next day.

"The bit of canned meat that the manager had tasted
had come from the left flank of a young heifer.
That heifer grazed away in the field,
wondering how it happened that she suddenly had a small hole in her left
flank."

Well, that must have been a remarkable canning factory. Perhaps you visited it and have a story to tell yourself?

From *Thai Tales: Folktales of Thailand* by Supaporn Vathanaprida, edited by Margaret Read MacDonald (Englewood, Colorado: Libraries Unlimited, 1994), pp. 6–7. Motif X1030 *Lie: remarkable building.*

The Rabbit Flood
A Folktale from Mexico

 5 minutes

There was a man who went out to clear a new field.
He worked very hard, cleared the brush all away, and cut down several trees.

The next day when he went back to plow the land . . .
the brush had grown back and the trees were standing again!

"What is this?"

Well, he started to work once more.
He cleared the brush away. He cut down the trees.
Then he went home.

Next morning . . . the same thing!
The brush had grown back, and the trees were all standing straight up again.

"What on earth can be causing this?"

The man went to work again clearing and cutting,
but this time he did not go home at the end of the day.
Instead, he hid himself in the forest nearby and kept watch.

Just before sunset, he saw a little animal come hopping up.
The animal started waving a wand around at the trees.

"Rise up! Trees! Back in place! Rise up!
Brush . . . back in place. Grow back!"

The man looked closely. It was a rabbit!
The rabbit was hopping all over the field.

He was waving his little wand at each bush and tree.
Those trees and bushes were jumping right back into the ground again!

"Hey! What are you doing? I'm trying to clear this land!"

The rabbit turned. "No more planting.
Leave it be. The world is coming to an end."

"Don't talk nonsense. I want to plant here."

"I'm telling you the truth," said the little rabbit.
"The world is coming to an end very soon.
But I can save you.
There is going to be an enormous flood.
Now go home and do what I tell you.
Build a wooden box big enough to hold your whole family.
Tell your wife to start making tortillas.
She must make a *lot* of tortillas.
Enough to last a very long time.
Gather in some beans and herbs for me too.
I will go with you.
I'll let you know when it is time."

And the little rabbit disappeared into the forest.

The man though the rabbit was probably talking nonsense.
But the rabbit *did* know how to do magic.
So the man didn't take any chances.
He went home and constructed a big wooden box.
It was big enough to hold his whole family.
And he told his wife to start making tortillas.
After a while everything was ready.

One day it started to rain.
"I wonder if this is the flood the little rabbit spoke about?"
But after a day, the rain stopped.

Then one day it started to rain again.
This time it was raining harder.

Pretty soon the little rabbit came running down from the mountain.
"It's time! Are you ready?"

They all climbed into the wooden box.
They piled up the tortillas, beans, and herbs inside and closed the door.
Just in time! It began to rain harder and harder.
Soon they could feel the box lifting on the waters.
It began to float. Higher and higher they rose on the waters.
They could peek out of a little hole in the top of the box.
It seemed like they were rising closer and closer to the sky.

Then one day they began to sink back down,
lower and lower, and at last they landed on the earth again.

The rabbit hopped out at once and began to nibble on some herbs he found.
But the man and his family were hungry for something other than tortillas.
They found a cow that had drowned and built a fire to cook some of the meat.

Up in Heaven, God smelled something burning.
"Fly down there and see what is going on," he said to some of his little angels.
"It smells like someone is cooking meat.
But whatever you do, don't eat any of it."

The angels flew right down. "What are you doing, man?"

"I'm cooking meat. Would you like a piece?"

"Oh no," said the angels.

"How about you, rabbit? Want a bite?"

"Not me!" The rabbit hopped off.

But the smell of that roasting meat did seem good.
Pretty soon the angels came closer.

"Maybe just a taste?" the man offered.

"Well . . . just a taste." The angels decided to try just a little piece.

It *was* good.

"Uh oh. God is going to be angry if he finds out we have been eating meat."

Those angels washed really well.
But the smell of the meat was still on them.
They rubbed themselves with some herbs to cover up the smell.

But that didn't even work.
When they reported back to God, he could smell what they had been doing.

"What have you been eating down there?"

"Oh . . . nothing . . ."

"Well, it doesn't smell like nothing. It smells like *meat*.
And since you like to eat meat so well, you will do that forever."

So saying, God turned those angels into vultures.
And sure enough . . . the vultures eat nothing but meat.

This unusual flood story is retold from "The World" in *Folktales of Mexico* by Americo Paredes (Chicago: University of Chicago Press, 1970), pp. 3–4. It was collected from Manuel Vidal Valderrama, an Otomí Indian, in Tlaxco, Puebla in 1963. He had learned it from the "old people," and his grandparents had spoken Náhuatl. Motifs are A522.1.2 *Rabbit as culture hero.* A1021 *Deluge: escape in boat (ark).* A1931 *Creation of vulture.* A2435.4.5.1 *Carrion as food of vultures.* B437.4 *Helpful rabbit.* C221 *Tabu: eating meat.* V236 *Fallen angels.* H1115.1 *Task: cutting down huge tree which magically regrows.* D1602.2 *Felled tree raises itself again.* MacDonald cites a Yoruba tale from West Africa with similar motif: D1487.3.1★ *Kin Kin, smallest forest bird, sings telling King of Forest to repair ravages of animals trying to build garden. Sings jungle back each night. Cat kills.*

The Magic Canoe

A Kamaiurá story from Brazil

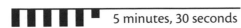 5 minutes, 30 seconds

A man decided to make a canoe.
Then he could go out to the deepest waters of the river to fish.

The man took bark from the jatobá tree.
From this he could make himself a canoe.
He worked hard on his canoe, and at last it was ready.

The man went home to rest that night, leaving the canoe in the clearing.
The next day he would drag it the long distance to the river.
Then he would fish.

In the morning the man was up early.
"We will have fresh fish today," he told his wife.
"My canoe is finished at last."

But when the man reached the clearing,
the canoe was gone.

"Someone has stolen my canoe."
He sat down and put his head in his hands.

But something was coming through the forest.

Sqwump . . . sqwump . . . sqwump . . . sqwump . . .

The bushes parted . . .
and his canoe poked its prow out.

During the night that canoe had grown eyes!
During the night it had grown a large mouth!
During the night that canoe had grown four stubby legs!

Sqwump . . . sqwump . . . sqwump . . . sqwump . . .

The canoe walked to the middle of the clearing.
Then . . . *SQWUMP!*
It sat down.

The man stared at his canoe.
This was *magic.*
Did he dare touch it?

Then one canoe paddle raised itself.
It motioned for the man to climb in.

Very cautiously, the man climbed into the canoe and sat down.
Nothing happened.

If it's a magic canoe, maybe I should give it a command, thought the man.
"Take me to the river!"

Slowly the canoe raised itself up on its stumpy little legs.
Then . . .

Sqwump . . . sqwump . . . sqwump . . . sqwump . . .

The canoe began to waddle down to the river.

Sqwump . . . sqwump . . . sqwump . . . shewwwwww . . .

The canoe slid into the water so easily.

It began to swim directly for the middle of the river.
Once it reached that spot the canoe stopped.
It waited.

Another command? thought the man.
"Catch fish!"

Immediately fish began to fly from the river into the boat.

FLAP! FLAP! FLAP! FLAP!

The man had to cover his head to protect himself from those flying fish.

Soon the canoe was full!

Then the canoe slowly turned its huge prow around,
and opened its enormous mouth.

Sluuurrrrp!

It swallowed down the entire boatload of fish!
Then it lay still in the water.

"Catch *more* fish?" hoped the man.

FLAP! FLAP! FLAP! FLAP!

The boat was filled once more.
Then the canoe turned itself slowly around and began to swim for shore.

Swwwwwwww . . . Sqwump! Sqwump! Sqwump!

It climbed from the water and began to stomp back up the path.
When the canoe reached the clearing it sat itself down.

SQWUMP!

The man took the fish from the canoe.
He stuffed them into his fish basket and hurried home.

"Wife, look at this!
We will not be hungry for a *long* time!"

They cleaned the fish and cooked some.
Others they put to dry for later.

The next morning the man took the biggest bag he could find.

"Wait until you see how many fish I bring home TONIGHT!
We can preserve them and SELL them!
We are going to be RICH!"

But when the man got to the clearing . . . his canoe was gone again.

"Oh no. My magic canoe is gone."

The man sat down and put his head in his hands.
But he soon heard a sound in the forest.

Sqwump . . . sqwump . . . sqwump . . . sqwump . . .

The bushes parted . . . and out came the canoe.

Sqwump . . . sqwump . . . sqwump . . . sqwump . . .

It stomped right to the middle of the clearing.

SQWUMP!

It sat itself down.

The man didn't wait to be invited.
He jumped right into the canoe and commanded:
"To the river!"

The canoe hoisted itself up onto its stumpy little legs.

Sqwump . . . sqwump . . . sqwump . . . sqwump . . .

It marched off down the path to the river.

Sqwump . . . sqwump . . . sqwump . . . Swwwwwwwww . . .

The canoe slid into the water.

It swam straight for the middle of the river.
Before it had even stopped, the man was ordering:
"Catch fish!"

FLAP! FLAP! FLAP! FLAP!

The canoe bottom was filled with fish.

"Catch *more* fish!"

FLAP! FLAP! FLAP! FLAP!

More fish came flying into the canoe.

"MORE! MORE FISH!"

And even *more* fish flew in.

The canoe was now so heavy with fish that its sides were barely above the
water.
The man was stuffing fish into his huge bag as fast as he could.

"MORE! MORE FISH!"

Suddenly everything stopped.
The canoe slowly turned its prow and stared at the man with its unfeeling
canoe eyes.
Then the man remembered that last time the canoe had eaten the first
batch of fish.

"Er . . . and some for you . . ." He tried hurriedly to pull a few fish from
his bag.
But it was too late.

The canoe stretched wide its huge jaws and . . .
Sluuurrrp!

It swallowed all the fish AND the man.

Deep in the Amazon forest live the Kamaiurá people.
They say this story is true.
Since the man did not survive, I am not sure who told the tale.
But the Kamaiurá *say* it is true.

Magic might come to one.
But the greedy will lose it all.

Retold from a Kamaiurá folktale, "Igaranhã: The
Enchanted Canoe" in *Xingu: The Indians, Their Myths*
by Orlando Villas Boas and Claudio Villas Boas (New
York: Farrar, Straus and Giroux, 1970), pp. 135–136.
Motifs are D1122 *Magic canoe.* D1523.2 *Self-propelling
(ship) boat.* Stith Thompson cites examples of self-pro-
pelling boats from Ireland, India, Breton tradition, the
Marquesas, Africa (Fang), and from native American
traditions. But none of them eat their owners! W151
Greed.

The Creature of the Night

A Brazilian Tale
Retold from Livia de Almeida

 5 minutes

Maria lived all by herself in a small house beside the shore.
Her life was hard . . . fetching water . . . drying fish . . .
Her only companion was a faithful dog who protected her from everything.
How she longed for a handsome man to pass by!
But this did not happen.

Then one evening, just after sunset, she heard a voice in the distance . . .

"Maria . . . Maria . . ."

It was a man's voice.
It was so low and mysterious.

And it was coming closer.
"Maria . . . Maria . . ."

Maria put on her lipstick.
She combed her hair.
She sat by the window and waited.

Closer and closer came the voice . . .
"Maria . . . Maria . . . Maria . . ."

She could see a dark shadow on her doorstep.
She waited for the knock . . .
and then her dog began to sing back.

"Go away!
If you look for Maria . . . Maria . . .
Maria is not here. Go away!"

"What?" Maria jumped up and flung open the door.
But the dark stranger was gone.

"Dog! Why did you do that?"
She kicked the poor dog.
"Don't ever do that again!"

The next day she tied her dog in the back yard.
She wrapped a rope tightly around the dog's jaws so it could not bark.

And that evening, just after sunset,
She heard . . .
"Maria . . . Maria . . ."
Coming closer and closer . . .
"Maria . . . Maria . . . Maria . . ."

She sat beside the window.
She waited.
She could see the shadow on her doorstep.
She waited for the knock . . .

But from the back yard the dog began to sing . . . through its closed muzzle.
"Go away! If you look for Maria . . . Maria . . .
Maria is not here.
Go away!"

"Oh!" The dark stranger was gone.

Maria ran into the back yard.
I am sad to tell you that she was in such a rage.
She killed her dear dog.
She buried the dog right there.

And next evening . . .
"Maria . . . Maria. . . ."
She was waiting by the window.
Waiting for the knock . . .
There was the shadow on her doorstep . . .

But . . . from underground . . . the dear dog still sang.
"Go away! If you look for Maria . . . Maria . . .
Maria is not here.
Go away!"

The dark stranger was gone.

Maria dug up that dog's body.
She made a huge fire and burnt the dog up.
Nothing was left but a pile of ashes.

The next evening . . .
"Maria . . . Maria. . . ."
She was by her window waiting.
There was no dog to warn off the dark stranger this time.

"Maria . . . Maria . . . Maria . . ."
Here was the dark shadow . . .
She waited for the knock . . .

But a soft song came from the back yard . . .
"Go away . . . If you look for Maria . . . Maria . . .
Maria is not here . . .
Go away . . ."

Even the dog's *ashes* were singing!
"No!" But the dark stranger had gone.

Maria gathered all of those ashes.
She carried them in a basket to the edge of the cliff.
And she tossed the ashes into the sea.

They were carried here and there . . . away . . . away . . .
The dog was gone for good.

The next night Maria bathed in scented water.
She put on her best dress.
She put on her lipstick.
She combed her long hair.
She sat by the window.

"Maria . . . Maria . . ."

Closer . . . and closer . . .
"Maria . . . Maria . . . Maria . . ."

Her heart was beating!
"Maria . . . Maria . . . Maria . . . Maria . . ."

The shadow was by her door.
She waited for the . . .
KNOCK! KNOCK! KNOCK!

She flung open the door!

And the creature of the night . . . came in.

Retold from "The Creature of the Night" by Livia de
Almeida in *Brazilian Folktales* by Livia de Almeida and
Ana Portella, edited by Margaret Read MacDonald
(Westport, Connecticut: Libraries Unlimited, 2006).
The story was collected in Maranhão, in the north of
Brazil. The original chant mixed Portuguese and
native words. This tale is similar to a British tale, "The
Hobyahs." MacDonald B332.1★ *Too watchful dog killed.*

Trickery

Trickster tales are popular the world over. "Fiddler's Gold" shows a Hungarian gypsy tricking the Devil. "That's the Way the World Goes" is a Br'er Rabbit tale in which he tricks —of course—Br'er Fox. "The Dog Market at Buda" is a well-known Hungarian tale telling of the historical King Mátyá and a trick he purportedly played on a rich man who in turn was trying to trick a poor fellow. This takes place in the "Buda" of Budapest.

For Hanukkah, try telling Naomi Baltuck's version of the traveler who tricks an innkeeper into a large feast by threatening to do "What Herschel's Father Did."

I love Masako Sueyoshi's little tale of an old woman who inadvertently frightens off two thieves by chanting sutras. Use a tiny metal gong when you tell this.

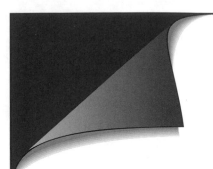

Fiddler's Gold

A Gypsy Folktale

5 minutes, 30 seconds, or longer, depending on length and frequency of your refrain

The gypsies in Europe often live a difficult life. At most towns they reach, the citizens are not happy to see them come. They are treated poorly and encouraged to move on as soon as possible. This may explain why the gypsy in our story was playing such a sad song on his violin and singing . . .

> As a prisoner I am guarded.
> At my right hand stalks my shadow.
> And my thoughts drag close behind me,
> like some harsh and cruel jailer.

It seemed that everywhere he went he was unwanted.
And so this sad song.

The song wafted out the open windows of the inn where the gypsy was playing.
It drifted down through the bulrushes along the river.
So sad was the song that the reeds and bulrushes became covered in teardrops.
They drooped over, wet as with dew.

And the Devil, who was residing just then in an old willow on the banks of the bog,
heard this plaintive singing too.

The Devil was so moved by this song that he became filled with compassion for the poor gypsy. The Devil certainly knew what it meant to be unloved. He resolved to cheer the poor gypsy up.

The gypsy had by now collected his pay for the music and was walking down the river path. As he walked along, he still sang:

> As a prisoner I am guarded.
> At my right hand stalks my shadow.
> And my thoughts drag close behind me,
> like some harsh and cruel jailer.

Suddenly a strange-looking man jumped out of the rushes just ahead of him.

"Don't stop singing!
Did I frighten you? Sorry about that!
I do enjoy your music."

"I was just startled." The gypsy looked closely at the strangely clothed man. He was wearing a very old-fashioned suit, smoking a large pipe, with a velvet hat on his head that did not quite cover two red horns!

"I'll bet you would be frightened if you found out that I was the Devil!"

The gypsy had not been fooled by the weird disguise. He knew exactly who he was dealing with.

"Even if you were the Devil himself, I would not be frightened. Why, the Devil must love a good tune as well as anyone."

"But I *am* the Devil!" And throwing off his cap, the Devil revealed those horns, of which the gypsy was already aware.

"Well, if you are really the Devil . . . grant me my wish."

"I will grant anything you wish. I expect you would like unlimited gold?"

"You can do that?"

"Yes, but it must be a bargain. In exchange you must give me the most precious thing you possess."

"That would be my violin."

"Yes."

"But what would you do with it?" asked the gypsy.

"I will play on it!" declared the Devil. "And when people hear, they will become so entranced that they will follow me wherever I wish to take them!"

The gypsy loved his violin. It was almost like his own life.
But still . . . unlimited gold?

"Well, show me the gold, and we will see!"

So the Devil showed the gypsy how to hop astride a bulrush, and the two rode off into the night sky. Far the Devil took the gypsy—as far as the waterfalls of Szamos-between-the-Mountains. That is how far they rode that night.

There the Devil bent over by a waterfall and scooped up a handful of sand. He handed it to the gypsy. It was gold!
Every grain was gold. Every pebble in the rivers here was gold.
Here was truly unlimited gold.

"May I at least say goodbye to my violin?"

The gypsy began to play one last time.
He played so sadly that the trees wept, the mountains wept . . . even the Devil wept.

And then he raised the violin to his lips, kissed it gently, and as he did so . . . he sucked all of the air out of the violin.

Then he handed it to the Devil.
The Devil took the violin and vanished.

For three days the gypsy took gold from this treasure site.
Truly he was rich.

But his heart was even sadder than before.
Trading music for gold is a bad bargain indeed.

On the third day, as he sat sadly on his pile of gold.
The Devil returned.

"What is wrong with this violin?
It does not draw people to me when I play.
Instead it drives them away with its squeaking!"

The gypsy smiled.
"Well sir, I said I would trade the violin.
But it is my soul that plays upon the strings and makes the music.
That I did not trade."

The Devil smiled ruefully.
"You have bested me, Gypsy.
Take back your violin.
It is useless to me. I can never play like you.

"But I have not lost this bargain entirely.
You have the gold and the violin.
But whenever you play . . . you will still draw people into my nets.
We shall see . . ."

They say that since that time the Devil no longer dances the waltz.
He only dances to gypsy *czardas*.
The gypsy, he receives gold whenever he plays.
And it is true that though the Devil was tricked by the gypsy,
men still fall into his net all the time.

> Reprise: sing the song once more to create a melancholy ending
> to the story.

As a prisoner I am guarded.
At my right hand stalks my shadow.
And my thoughts drag close behind me,
like some harsh and cruel jailer.

Retold from a Hungarian folktale, "How a Gypsy
Cheated the Devil," collected by in *A Book of Gypsy
Folk-Tales* by Dora E. Yates (London: Phoenix House,
1948), pp. 101–104. Also available in a Barnes &
Noble reprint as *Gypsy Folk-Tales* (1995). I do not
find this exact tale cited in Stith Thompson, though it
is related to F473.6.9 *Spirit plays man's fiddle at night*.
And the Devil's association with the fiddle is legion:
G303.0.5.8 *Devil takes violinist when he needs a good fiddler in hell*. England. K606.1.3 *Fiddler in hell breaks
string, must return to earth to repair*. G303.9.8.2 *Devil
plays fiddle at wedding*. G303.25.17.2 *A musician engaged
to play for the night-spirits (devils) dances*. No music was
given in my source; create a haunting melody of your
own if you wish.

That's the Way the World Goes

A Folktale from the American South
Retold from Marilyn Ribe

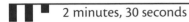 2 minutes, 30 seconds

One day the animals all went out to clear ground for a new cornfield.
It was very hard work, and the sun was hot.
After a couple hours of this,
Br'er Rabbit was looking for an excuse to get some shade.
"Oh! I've got a thorn in my paw!" he hollered.
"I've got to go tend it."
And he took off looking for a cool place to rest.

What should he find but a *well*.
"Oh now . . . *that* looks cool.
I'm just going to climb in one of these buckets and take a nap."

A bucket was hanging just inside the well.
It seemed really cool in there.
So without another thought, Br'er Rabbit jumped right into one of those buckets.

"Whoops!" His weight, of course, pulled the bucket down.
He felt himself riding deeper and deeper into that hole.
Then suddenly—*Splash!*—the bucket landed in the water . . .
with Br'er Rabbit inside.

Was he ever scared!
He knew that if he made one wrong move,
that bucket would turn over and dump him into the cold, cold water.
And that was cooler than he hoped to get.

Now, Br'er Fox always keeps an eye on Br'er Rabbit.
So when Br'er Rabbit had sneaked away from the work crew . . .
Br'er Fox followed after him.

What did he see but that rabbit disappearing down a well!

"He is up to something," thought Bre'r Fox.
"I'll bet Br'er Rabbit has his money hid down there in that hole.
Well, he can't outwit me!"

Br'er Rabbit was shaking like crazy down in that bucket.
He was starting to say his prayers real good.

Suddenly Br'er Fox's head loomed over the well opening.
"Hey there, Br'er Rabbit! What you up to down there?" hollered Br'er Fox.

Br'er Rabbit was always one to be quick with his thinking.
"Oh . . . just fishing, Br'er Fox. Just fishing."

"What on earth are you fishing for down in that well?"

"Why . . . I'm fishing for suckers, Br'er Fox. Yes, that's it.
I'm fishing for suckers."

"Have you caught many, Brer Rabbit?"

"Well it appears I'm just about to," replied Brer Rabbit.

Br'er Fox never liked to be left out of anything.
"Can I come down and fish with you, Br'er Rabbit?"

"No problem at all, Br'er Fox.
Just jump in the other bucket there and come on down."

Now of course these buckets were hung like a pulley.
If one went down . . . the other came up.

But that foolish fox jumped right in.
As he began sinking into the well . . .
Br'er Rabbit's bucket was slowly raised *out* of the well.

As they passed mid'way, Br'er Rabbit waved to Br'er Fox.

"Goodbye, Br'er Fox!
Take care your clothes!
That's the way the world goes.
Some goes up, and some goes down.
You'll get to the bottom all safe and sound."

Br'er Rabbit ran back to the field and told the folks that owned that well:
"You better run quick! Bre'r Fox is down in your well muddying it all up!"

Then he ran ahead of them back to the well and hollered down to
B'rer Fox:
"Here comes a man with a great big gun.
When they haul you up, better jump and run!"

And that is just what Br'er Fox did.

Back in 1965 I heard children's librarian Marilyn Ribe tell this story
often at King County Library System programs. I always loved the way
she delivered the line, "That's the way the world goes!" She shaped the
tale from "Old Mr. Rabbit, He's a Good Fisherman" in *The Complete
Tales of Uncle Remus* by Joel Chandler Harris (Boston: Houghton
Mifflin, 1955), pp. 50–53. It originally appeared in *Uncle Remus: His
Songs and His Sayings,* first published in 1880. The story is widely told
throughout Europe, Latin America, and the United States. Usually the
protagonists are a fox and a wolf, rather than a fox and a rabbit. Stith
Thompson Motif K651 *Wolf descends into well in one bucket and rescues fox
in the other.* Type 32 *Wolf Descends into Well in One Bucket and Rescues the
Fox in the Other.* The Antti Aarne Type Index cites sources for this from
Germany, Spain, Finland, Sweden, Denmark, Italy, Hungary, Slovenia,
Russia, Greece, Argentina, and Chile. Stith Thompson's motif-index adds
sources from England, Pennsylvania, South Carolina, and the Joel
Chandler Harris variant from Georgia. MacDonald indexes this as
K651.0.1★ *Fox and Rabbit.* MacDonald and Sturm add a French version
of the tale (fox and wolf).

The Dog Market at Buda
A Folktale from Hungary

 2 minutes, 30 seconds

A poor man met his rich neighbor on the road.
The rich neighbor was returning from the market in Buda with a bag full of coins.

"It looks like you did good business today," said the poor man.

The rich man thought he would have some fun at the expense of this poor man.
"Oh yes," said the rich man. "I just sold a pack of dogs to the king.
He is paying a lot of money for dogs, you know.
There is quite a Dog Market in Buda."

And the rich man went on, chuckling to himself.

The poor man was excited. He knew where there were a lot of stray dogs.
The next day, the poor man worked hard and rounded up quite a pack of dogs.
It was hard to herd them into town and over the bridge into Buda. But he did it.

Here he came to the castle gate.
His dogs were barking loudly.
They were racing in circles, getting their ropes tangled up.
But the poor man was dragging them forward,
right through the gates and into the courtyard of the castle.
The guards hurried up to send the crazy poor man away.

But King Matthias was looking on from his window.
Now King Matthias was called Matthias the Just.
And there was a reason for this. He was an unusually wise man.

"There must be some strange story behind this poor man with his dogs,"
thought King Matthias. And he called for the man to be brought to him.

As soon as he heard the story of the "Dog Market in Buda," the king realized
that the rich neighbor had been playing a cruel trick on the poor man.
"Well," said King Matthias, "you are in luck.
Today does happen to be the day of the Dog Market here in Buda."
And the king gave the poor man a bag of gold coins for his dogs.

As soon as the poor man returned home, he went to his rich neighbor to
thank him for the advice.

"Now I am wealthy, too!" said the man. "And it is all because of your kind
advice about the Dog Market."

The very next day, the rich man hurried around town buying all the dogs
he could find.
It was with great difficulty that he managed to drag all of those howling
dogs into Buda and up to the castle. But he did it.

When King Matthias heard the yapping of dogs in his courtyard, he knew
at once what he would see. And sure enough, he looked out the window
and there was the rich man . . . surrounded by dogs.

"Guard!" called King Matthias.
"Throw out this man and his dogs!"

"But I have come for the Dog Market in Buda!" shouted the rich man.

"Well," said King Matthias,
"you are too late.
The Dog Market in Buda only took place once!"

Retold from "One-Time Dog Market at Buda" in *One-Time Dog Market At Buda and Other Hungarian Folktales* by Irma Molnár (North Haven, Connecticut: Linnet Books, 2001), pp. 17–20 and from "A Deal that Went to the Dogs" in *Folktales of Hungary,* edited by Linda Dégh (Chicago: University of Chicago Press, 1965), pp. 168–170. Dégh tells us that this incident took place between 1460 and 1470, during the reign of King Mátyá the Righteous. Her version was from László Márton, a farmhand from Bukovina, who wrote it down early in the twentieth century. This is related to Type 1689 *Two Presents to the King.* In that tale one man takes a beet to the king and is rewarded. His rival takes a fine horse and is given the beet. Buda and Pest were once separate towns on each side of the Danube River. Since the river was bridged in 1896, the unified metropolis is Budapest. The saying is still common in Hungary: "The Dog Market happened only once in Buda." This is used when someone misses an opportunity that will not come again. Many stories are told about King Matthias the Just, a favorite historical king of Buda.

What Herschel's Father Did

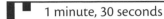

A Jewish Folktale
Retold by Naomi Baltuck

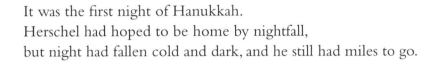

1 minute, 30 seconds

It was the first night of Hanukkah.
Herschel had hoped to be home by nightfall,
but night had fallen cold and dark, and he still had miles to go.

First things first.
He went to an inn and asked the innkeeper for something to eat.
But the innkeeper could tell that Herschel had no money.
"No," said the innkeeper. "There is no food left."

"No food left? On the first night of Hanukkah?
Surely you can spare one little latke, or a bite of applesauce?"

"Nothing!" said the innkeeper.

"Not a crumb? Not a drop?"

"Not a crumb! Not a drop!"

"That does it!" muttered Herschel.
"If I don't get something to eat, then I will do what my father did!"

"Well, do it outside," said the innkeeper.

"You don't believe me, but I will do it.
I'll do what my father did!"

The innkeeper was getting nervous.
He didn't know what Herschel's father had done,
but he was certain that he didn't want Herschel to do it to him.

"Yes . . . that's what I'll do," said Herschel, pacing back and forth. "And no one here is going to stop me."

The innkeeper was so frightened that he backed into his kitchen. He came back with a tray laden with food left over from his own dinner— potato latkes, applesauce, fruit, and cheese.

He filled Herschel's plate and poured him some drink quickly, as if his life depended on it.

Herschel ate every crumb, and he drank every drop. At last Herschel smiled, loosened his belt, and pushed away from the table.

"Now are you happy, Herschel?" asked the innkeeper.

"Yes, thank you very much."

"You're not angry?"

"Not at all."

"Then tell me," asked the innkeeper. "What did your father do when he didn't get something to eat?"

"What else could he do? He went to bed *hungry!*"

This is the story as Seattle storyteller and author Naomi Baltuck shared it with the Seattle Storyteller's Guild in December 2002. Naomi writes that she adapted this Jewish story into a Hanukkah setting when she needed more Hanukkah tales for a program. Naomi has created a delightfully tellable version of this old tale. Motif J1340 *Retorts from hungry persons.*

The Mouse Sutra

A Japanese Folktale
Retold from Masako Sueyoshi

 5 minutes

There was once an old woman who lived all alone.
One evening a young student monk named Kozosan came to her home.
"It is too dark for me to reach the temple tonight," said the boy.
"Could I please stay the night at your house?"

The kind old woman took him in.
She fed the young monk sweet potato soup for his supper.

After the meal, she spoke to him:
"Today is the anniversary of my husband's death.
Would you please pray a sutra for him?
I don't know any sutras myself. Please pray for him."

Kozosan did not have experience in praying sutras yet.
But he didn't want to disappoint the old woman.
So he sat down in front of the family altar and pretended to pray just like
the priests did.

Ching! Ching! he hit a small metal gong with a little stick.

He cleared his throat. What could he say?

Just then he saw two little mice peeking out from the wall.
Chorro . . . chorro . . . chorro . . .
Their little paws scratched along the floor.

So he began to chant.

"*On chorro . . . chorro . . . chorrorin.*
Mairare sooro.
They are coming."

Then he hit the gong. *Ching!*

The old woman nodded. And the young monk continued.

"*On chorro chorro chorrorin.*
Nozokare sooro.
They are peeking."
Ching!

The mice began to chatter to each other and he had his next verse.

"*On chorro chorro chorrorin.*
Sasayaki sooro.
They are whispering."
Ching!

The mice ran back to their hole, and Kozosan played his last sutra.

"*On chorro chorro chorrorin.*
Kaerare sooro.
They are leaving."
Ching!

He finished the sutra.

The old woman was delighted! Such an *easy* sutra!
"I can sing that myself!" she thought.

When Kozosan had left, the old woman sat down in front of the family altar and began to chant. She was glad to have a sutra she could say herself now.

Just at that moment, two thieves approached the old woman's house. They were about to slide open the shoji door and enter when . . . they heard the old woman muttering.

"*On chorro . . . chorro . . . chorrorin.*
Mairare sooro.
They are coming."
Ching!

What? Had she seen them approaching?

The thieves peeked in through a hole in her shoji door.

"*On chorro chorro chorrorin.*
Nozokare sooro.
They are peeking."
Ching!

"She must have seen us come in!"

"*On chorro chorro chorrorin.*
Sasayaki sooro.
They are whispering."
Ching!

"She saw us! She knows we are here!
We'd better get out quickly before she calls for help."

And the two thieves crept away from the house and hurried off. Behind them they heard:

"*On chorro chorro chorrorin.*
Kaerare sooro.
They are leaving."
Ching!

The thieves started running as fast as they could away from that old woman's house.
And of course they never did return.

To this day, the old woman peacefully prays her special sutra every night.

"*On chorro chorro chorrorin . . .*"
CHING!

<hr />

This story is retold by Japanese teller Masako Sueyoshi and appears in her Japanese storytelling collection, *Mukashibanashi World-e-Yokoso!* (Tokyo: Isseisha, Inc., 2005), pp. 44–47. It is nice to tell this with a tiny gong to make the *ching!* sound. N612 *Numbskull talks to himself and frightens robbers away.* MacDonald's *Storyteller's Sourcebook* (1982) cites versions of this story from Burma, Korea, and the Grimms' "Dr. Know-it-all" tale. MacDonald and Sturm's *Storyteller's Sourcebook 1983–1999* (2002) lists versions from Greece, Persia, and the Appalachian story of "Old One-Eye." Stith Thompson's *Motif-Index of Folk-Literature* cites versions from India and Turkey.

Lessons
to Be Learned

After reading several Russian tales of Djadja Bear and his friends, I began to tell the story of "Little Fox's Village." It is my own creation, not a folktale. But I have used stock folktale characters to make a point I think needs making: don't litter!

"The Queen and the Peasant Wife" is a traditional tale from India of switched wives. The queen learns her lesson—just as well as the switched wives of today's reality shows learn theirs.

The Egyptian tale "The Household Snake" shows a mother snake who plots her revenge for cruel boys who mistreat her young . . . and then relents.

The folklorist Vance Randolph collected many tales from the Ozarks region of Arkansas and Missouri. He heard "Toad-Frog" in 1929. I try to keep the language very close to the way he heard and transcribed it.

"The Papercut Woman" is a Chinese tale that passed through many hands to reach us. Collected by a Chinese researcher, retold by a Harvard researcher to a Seattle storyteller teaching in Lanzhou, China . . . and retold by her to this author at a workshop in Mahasarakham, Thailand! A wonderful tale of a woman's discovery of her self.

And last of all in this book comes "Singing Together." I love this Ukrainian tale of the value of a song . . . and perhaps also the value of a story.

Little Fox's Village
An Original Tale

4 minutes

Little Fox and Djadja Bear and Djadja Boar and Djadja Rabbit made a village together.
Little Fox built herself a house.
Djadja Bear built himself a house.
Djadja Boar built himself a house.
And Djadja Rabbit built himself a house.

On the first day after they had moved in,
Little Fox looked out her front door and saw Djadja Rabbit eating a carrot.
When Djadja Rabbit finished eating,
he just tossed the carrot top out into the street.

"Djadja Rabbit, do you really mean to throw your garbage into the street?" called Little Fox.

"Why not?" replied Djadja Rabbit.
"What's the problem?"
And he went back into his house.

The next day Little Fox saw Djadja Boar strolling by eating an apple.
When Djadja Boar finished, he just tossed his apple core into the street.

"Djadja Boar? Do you really want to be throwing garbage around in the street?" asked Little Fox.

"No problem," said Djadja Boar. "What does it matter?"

The very next day Little Fox noticed Djadja Bear tossing empty honeycombs out into the street.

"But Djadja Bear? Why are you dirtying up our street?" asked Little Fox.

"What does it matter?" said Djadja Bear. "Just walk around it."

Things went on like this for one whole week.
Now Little Fox had to wade through garbage every time she left her house.

Still Djadja Bear, Djadja Boar, and Djadja Rabbit thought nothing about tossing down any garbage they happened to have in their hands and just walking off.
After a month the street was so full of trash that Little Fox could barely get by.

Then one day, when their village was just three months old,
Little Fox opened her door and shrieked.
The mountain of garbage had grown so high that she could not even get out of her house!

Little Fox packed up her things,
climbed out her back window,
and went deeper into the forest to build a new house.

She wasn't there long before Djadja Rabbit came trundling along with his belongings in a handbarrow.

"Couldn't get out my front door this morning.
Mind if I build beside you?"

And Djadja Rabbit began a new house.

Since Djadja Boar and Djadja Bear were bigger,
it was another week before they found that they too were trapped under the mound of garbage.

Then along they came to build new houses too.
Soon a lovely new, clean village had grown up in the forest.

One day Little Fox looked out her door.
Djadja Rabbit had just finished his morning carrot and was about to toss the carrot top into the street.

"STOP RIGHT THERE!" ordered Little Fox.
"Don't you remember our *last* village?
It *does* make a difference where you throw your garbage.
Now walk around behind your house and start yourself a compost heap."

So Djadja Rabbit and Djadja Bear and Djadja Boar each found a place to compost their garbage. And from then on no one dropped even one piece of trash in the streets of their town.
So they lived there happily for many, many years.

Created after telling a Russian folktale about Djadja Rabbit, Djadja Bear, Djadja Boar, and Little Fox. This obviously didactic little piece makes use of these stock folk characters.

The Queen and the Peasant Wife

A Folktale from India

 5 minutes

When the king and queen were out traveling one day,
they passed by the hut of a poor peasant.

The man and his wife were clothed in rags.
Their filthy children were playing in the muddy yard.

"Look at those poor people," said the king.
"God seems to have abandoned them."

"God has nothing to do with it," retorted the queen.
"The woman of that house is no good.
So all their labor is wasted.
Even if they worked day and night, they could not escape poverty."

"That cannot be true," said the king.

"I will make you a wager.
Let me manage this peasant's house for six months.
Let the peasant's wife go and take my place in the palace for six months.
You will see the difference."

So the two women exchanged places.

The queen took one look at the peasant's filthy house.
Then she rolled up her sleeves and got to work.

First she bathed the smelly children,
washed their clothes,

dressed them properly,
and instructed them how to play without getting into the mud.

Next she hauled out all the refuse piled inside the house,
swept, scrubbed,
cleaned all the pots,
tossed out all the rancid foodstuffs,
and washed the beddings.

Then she drew beautiful *rangoli* designs on the floor,
brought in flowers for the gods, and lit incense.

When the husband came home that night
She instructed him to go for a bath!
Then she washed *his* clothes,
trimmed his hair,
and informed him that from now on he would take a bath each day
and would start each day in clean clothing.

"And," she added, "you must work every day.
If you have nothing to do on the farm,
Go to town and look for work.
And even if you find no work there,
do not come home without picking up something to bring back.
Even if it is only a stick for the fire . . . each day you much accomplish
something."

As the days passed, the man brought home a few coins each day.
The queen put these away in a secret pot.
And after a while, she had enough to buy a few nice things to make the
home more livable.

She cooked well, and soon the man and his family began to look healthy
and happy.

In the meanwhile, the peasant wife was wreaking havoc in the palace.
She never picked up a thing.
The palace was soon littered with filth.
She was too lazy even to order the servants to tidy things.

When she did approach the servants it was to shout at them and order
them to bring her this and that sweet to eat.
She caused the servants such grief that they stayed well out of her sight.

When the king came near her quarters he was appalled.
There were bits of gnawed food rotting everywhere.
Soiled linen was piled in the corners.
And she had raised such discord in the household . . .
everyone was now shouting at everyone else!
He hoped the six months would pass quickly.

One day the peasant couldn't find any work.
On the way home, he noticed a dead snake lying in the road.
"Well, it is *something*," he thought.
So he carried it home.

"Well, you did try," said the queen.
And she tossed the dead snake aside.

Now just then Garuda, that magical bird, was flying overhead.
A necklace of pearls and rubies dangled from his beak,
something he had carried off from a palace.
Garuda is a fierce enemy of snakes.
So when Garuda saw the snake, he went into a steep dive to snatch it up.
But in doing this, he dropped the necklace.
Hearing the beating of wings, the queen rushed out.
There was a glittering necklace! She knew its worth.
The husband was sent off to town at once to sell it.
With the money from that sale, she was able to buy a new house, some
land, and cattle.

When the six months had passed the king came hurrying to deliver the
peasant wife home.
But here was a fine farm.
There were clean, well-behaved children
and a hard-working husband looking after his cattle.
The king was amazed.

"But everything is a *mess* in the palace," said the king.
"Everyone is fighting.
The place is covered in filth.
And this woman has spent so much I am nearly in ruins!"

"Then I win the wager," laughed the queen.
"You see, the woman of the house is like Lakshmi, the Goddess of Good Fortune.
Even in the poorest household,
a woman who looks after her home and cares well for her children and her husband will attract Lakshmi to that household.
And good fortune will follow.

"And even to the most wealthy home,
a women who takes no care for her house or family
will bring disaster."

So the peasant woman was put back into her own house.
But not before the queen gave her a few words of advice.

And the king and his queen hurried home to take care of the disasters that woman had left behind!

Retold from "A Flowering Tree and Other Oral Tales from India" by A.K. Ramanujan (Berkeley: University of California Press, 1997), pp. 94–96. A very sweet, but longer telling appears there. Related motifs are: P411.1.1 *Peasant and wife in hut near castle as contrasts to king and queen.* N134 *Persons effect change of luck.* N134.1.2 *Wife brings bad luck to the husband's family.* W20 *Other favorable traits of character.* MacDonald W48★ *Industry.*

The Household Snake

A Folktale from Egypt

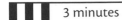

3 minutes

In Cairo, Egypt, it is said that snakes live in the houses of families especially favored by God. These guardian serpents make certain that no other reptiles enter the home, and they protect the place against evil. Since the guardian snake comes out mainly at night—or in secret when everyone is out—it is seldom seen.

But sometimes the children of the snake do not understand that they must take care not to be observed by the family.

It was in the Cairo house known as Beit al-Kretliya that this story took place. One day when the owner, Hajj Muhammad, was out, two little snake children wriggled out onto the floor and began to explore. It didn't take long for the two sons of Hajj Muhammad to notice these creatures. At once the boys pounced on the snakes, caught them, and began to experiment with the poor things, twisting them this way and that. Then tying each snake with a string, the boys began to drag them around the patio behind them.

The mother snake soon missed her children and began to creep about searching for them. There they were! Being mistreated by those two boys! The mother snake was furious. No more would she protect *this* household!

A large *zir* water jar was standing in the courtyard. The mother snake slithered up onto this jar and meanly spat poison into the water. "They will mistreat my children? Then the members of this house will drink my poison!"

Just then Hajj Muhammad returned home. He was horrified when he saw what his sons were doing with the young snakes. "Stop that at once! Don't you know how to behave with God's creatures? These little snakes belong to the serpent who protects our home. You must let them go at once and beg her forgiveness. Don't ever do a thing like this again!"

The mother snake saw all this and was relieved to see her released sons come wriggling back to her. But now she was worried about her own hasty actions. If Hajj Muhammad or any of his household drank from the *zir* water they might die. She had just heard Hajj Muhammad call to the servant girl to bring him a cup of fresh water. She had to think fast.

Quickly the mother serpent moved up and around the water jar. Then, coiling her body around and around it, she began to squeeze. That snake squeezed with every ounce of strength she had in her body. She squeezed . . . she squeezed . . . and suddenly . . .

The jar broke! The poisoned water gushed out onto the floor.

At the sound of the breaking jar, the household rushed to see what had happened. They did not see the snake disappearing back into her hole.

But here was the *zir* . . . broken into ninety-nine pieces. They were amazed. Because of this magical number, they believed the jar to have been broken by a *djinn*.

It was never known to them that their lives had actually been saved by the benevolent household serpent.

A version of this story appears as "The Benevolent Serpent" in *Egyptian Legends and Stories* by M.V. Seton-Williams (London: The Rubicon Press, 1988), pp. 121–122. An earlier version is found in *Legends of the Beit al-Kretliya* by R.G. Gayer-Anderson (Ipswich: East Anglian Daily Times, 1951). The tale was collected by Gayer-Anderson in Cairo. Seton-Williams tells us that this legend is connected with the ancient house of Beit al-Kretliya, which was located next to the Ibn Talun Mosque. The *zir* is a large earthen pot with a pointed bottom. It rests on a wooden frame and is a fixture in courtyards. A *djinn* is of course a supernatural creature. The notion of a snake as a guardian house spirit is held in several cultures. I have seen mention of this in West Africa, and my host in Northeastern Thailand treated her yard cobra with this same respect. B593.1 *Snake as house-spirit.* Stith Thompson gives only one citation. This is related to B521.1 *Animal warns against poison* and B514.3 *Snake gives man antidotes for poison.*

Toad-Frog
A Folktale from Missouri

 5 minutes, 30 seconds

These two brothers were named Charley and Bud.
Now Charley was just plumb mean.
But Bud was a gentle, sweet fellow.

Only problem was . . . Bud could not talk.
So Charley got to do all the talking for the both of them.

Now three girls lived up the road.
And those girls liked to go swimming in the pond.
They didn't know anyone was watching . . . thought they had it all to
themselves.
But Charley would hide in the bushes down there and spy on them.
One day Charley heard them telling as to how their father had hid his
money in a cave way back in the woods.

It wasn't long before Charley told Bud that were going to go for a hike
back in the woods. Sure enough . . . there was a cave.

Inside, Charley started digging around and digging around . . .
And he found an iron skillet all wrapped up. It was packed full of gold coins.
It belonged to the father of those girls.
This was the hidden money they had talked about.
But Charley pretended otherwise.

"Probably Spanish gold," he told Bud. "Been hid in here for a long time.
We'll just take it home with us. Finders keepers."

But Bud started fingering the gold coins . . . and he saw they weren't *old*
coins at all.

So he knew the gold belonged to somebody. And that they shouldn't be taking it.
Charley could see that his brother was guessing the truth.

Charley wanted that gold. And he wanted the gold more than he wanted a brother.
So he raised that heavy skillet to whack Bud over the head.

But just then he heard a little squeak of a laugh.
He whirled around and . . .
There sat a little dried-up looking old fellow smoking a pipe.
The fellow was rocking back and forth and laughing at him.

"Who are you?" hollered Charley. "And what are you doing in this cave?"

"I'm the *king* of these parts," says the little man. "And I live in this cave."

"And furthermore," says he, "I don't take kindly to boys that sneak around staring at girls while they swim. And I especially don't take kindly to boys who steal gold and think about bashing in their brother's head with a frying pan!"

Well, Charley was scared pretty bad.
But he knew Bud couldn't talk and couldn't tell on him.

So he just glared at the little dried-up fellow and snorted,
"You don't scare me.
You ain't no king at all.
You're nothing but a little toad-frog!"

"Toad-frog?" said the little man.
"Toad-frog? Well I'd say *you* are the toad-frog!"

And he pointed his skinny little finger at Charley.
Then he made a little *pop* noise with his mouth, like he was spitting out a persimmon seed.

And with that little *pop* Charley dropped to the ground.
He began to kick and holler.
And then he began to wiggle and grunt.
He seemed to be getting smaller and smaller.
Charley was shrinking right before Bud's eyes.
His jeans were just falling off him.
And as he got smaller and smaller . . . Charley started turning greener and
greener . . .

"Toad-frog yourself!" hollered the old king.
"Git for the creek, toad-frog!"

And off went that poor toad-frog Charley, hopping over the rocks like they
hurt his feet, until he plopped into the creek.

"Well," the little dried-up king turned to Bud. "What do you have to say
for yourself?"

And Bud opened his mouth . . . and started in talking! Just like that.
He told the king how they'd dug up the money, but he saw it wasn't
Spanish gold and figured it didn't belong to them.

"Well bury it back, then," said the little king. "And don't you ever tell a
soul what you saw here today. Understand? If you tell *anybody* about this
you will never be able to stop talking again." And the little old fellow
popped down a hole and disappeared . . . just like a groundhog.

Bud went home, and when folks saw that he could talk at last, they were
just tickled to death. They forgot all about wondering where Charley was.

When they finally got around to missing Charley, Bud said he didn't have
any idea what had become of him. And he stuck to that story.

So Charley was gone. And the years passed. And Bud married and had kids
and grandkids and lived a real good life.

But when he was dying . . . he said he had something to tell.

And he told this story. Folks couldn't believe it was true. Figured it was the ramblings of an old man.

But at the very minute Bud died, a creek broke out up above the house and came burbling down the holler. And ever since that day the creek has never stopped burbling.

Some say it is Bud. And that he has to keep talking and talking . . . just like the old king cursed him to do.

Tourists call that creek "Talking River" because it chatters so loud. But local folks call it something else. They call it "Bud's Creek." And they figure maybe Bud isn't exactly dead. . . . Maybe he just turned into a creek that never shuts up.

Retold from "Talking River" in "Bedtime Stories from Missouri" by Vance Randolph (*Western Folklore,* v. X, no. 1, January 1951, pp. 8–10). Collected from Mr. William Hatton of Columbia, Missouri, July 1929. He told Randolph that he had heard the story in Lawrence County, Missouri, around 1905. Hatton told Randolph, "There's some dirty words in this story, but I will leave them out if you're going to write it down on paper." I left a few more of them out in my retold version! F715.1 *Extraordinary source of river.* D196 *Man transformed to toad.*

The Papercut Woman

Drawn from an Oral History from China
Retold from JonLee Joseph

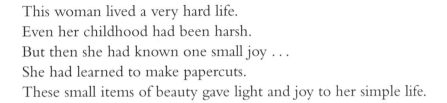

1 minute, 30 seconds

This woman lived a very hard life.
Even her childhood had been harsh.
But then she had known one small joy . . .
She had learned to make papercuts.
These small items of beauty gave light and joy to her simple life.

But adulthood had brought her much grief.
She had borne ten children,
but only three had lived to become adults.
Her husband abused her,
and his family treated her also with scorn.
There was little happiness in this woman's life.
She could accept the harshness of her surroundings,
but the abuse of her husband and in-laws made her life truly miserable.

One dark night, she was walking home alone.
It had been an exhausting day, and the woman was tired.
Somehow she slipped and fell into the roadside ditch.
She lay there all night. Perhaps no one even missed her.
But in the morning her body was discovered.
When they hauled her out of the ditch, it seemed that she was still alive . . .
But she was without consciousness.

She was brought to the doctor, who slapped her hard to wake her up.
But it was no use. For days she lay in a coma.
And then one day she sat up. She looked around.
But this was not the woman who had fallen into the ditch . . .
This was an entirely new creature!
"I am The Papercut Woman!" she declared boldly.

"I am the one who makes papercuts.
And it is I who can heal with my papercuts."

The woman had a totally new personality.
She had *become* The Papercut Woman.
Now she was confident and demanding.
She would accept no abuse from her husband or her in-laws.
The creation of papercuts became her life work.
She would design special papercuts to bring healing to sick people.
And these did help them recover.

She became famous throughout her region as The Papercut Woman.
And in her old age, she was given great respect.
She was honored as an amazing artisan of this folk craft.

This story was told to me by JonLee Joseph, a teacher at Mahasarakham University in Mahasarkham, Thailand. JonLee had heard this story from Julie Taylor-Brousseau, a Harvard researcher whom she met in Lanzhou, China. The source was given as: Li, Xiaojiang, ed., *Rang niren ziji shuo hua: wenhua xunzong [Let women speak on their own: searching for cultural traces]* (Beijing: Sanlian chuban shudian [Shanlian Publishing Co.], 2003). This is a three-volume collection of women's oral histories. Thanks to JonLee for sharing this tale.

Singing Together
A Ukrainian Folktale

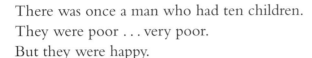 5 minutes

There was once a man who had ten children.
They were poor . . . very poor.
But they were happy.

Every evening after supper they would gather around and sing.

> "Oh, we love to sing together!
> We're so happy just singing together!
> We don't need money.
> We don't need gold.
> We just need to sing together!"

They would sing one song after another . . . on and on into the night.

Now right next door, as so often happens in these stories,
there lived a rich man.
This rich man *hated* the sound of their singing.
Every night . . .

> "Oh, we love to sing together . . ."

He could not stand it.

"What do *they* have to be singing about?
I am the rich person around here!"

One day in early December the rich man could stand it no longer.
"They don't need money?
They don't need gold?
We will see about that!"

The rich man took a large bag of gold from his treasury.
He carried it next door to the poor man and knocked.

When the poor man opened the door, the rich man said,
"You have no idea how annoying your singing is!
I have a bargain for you.
I would like to buy your songs.
Here is a bag of gold for you.
Do not sing anymore."

The poor man took the huge bag of gold.
What he could not do with this gold!
There was enough there to keep his family in comfort for years.
"Thank you."

He took the gold inside and closed the door.
"No more singing here," he told his family.
"We won't be singing anymore.
We have sold our songs for all this gold."

That night after dinner,
The family did not sing.

And the next night.
And the next.

After a week,
the poor man noticed that the light had gone out of his children's eyes.

A second week passed.
There was quiet in the house now.
The children seldom even talked to each other.

A third week passed.
The poor man saw that his children walked with stooped shoulders.
They went about their days without joy.

On Christmas Eve the man took the bag of gold from the spot where he had hidden it.

"What fine presents I could buy for the children with this gold," he thought. "Christmas will be poor enough in our house tomorrow."

He held the gold in his hands for a long while.
Then he left the house.

On Christmas morning the rich man was awakened by such a sound from next door!

> "Oh, we love to sing together!
> We're so happy just singing together!
> We don't need money.
> We don't need gold.
> We just need to sing together!"

"What?" the rich man exclaimed. "I bought their songs!"

The rich man raced out his front door . . .
And stumbled over a bag on his front step.
A bag of gold.
Returned.

And next door the man and his children were enjoying the best present anyone could ever want . . .
a joyful heart.

> "Oh, we love to sing together!
> We're so happy just singing together!
> We don't need money.
> We don't need gold.
> We just need to sing together!"

Retold from a Ukrainian folktale, "Sad Songs and Gay," found in *Ukrainian Folk Tales* compiled by Volodimir Boyko (Kiev: Dnipro, 1981) pp. 387–388. C481 Singing Tabu.